Barbara Jacobs is an ex-teacher who has been writing full-time for more than ten years. She has contributed regularly to a wide range of teenage magazines and is the author of three previous books published in the Corgi Freeway list. These are STICK, which was serialized in *Jackie* magazine and shortlisted for the Guardian Award and the Federation of Children's Book Groups Children's Award, JUST HOW FAR? and NOT REALLY WORKING.

LOVE'S A PAIN is a collection of some of her best short stories, including some first published in top teen magazines *Just Seventeen*, *Mizz* and *Blue Jeans*, as well as stories specially written for this book.

Praise for Barbara Jacobs's books:

'This book deals sensitively, humorously and realistically with a number of issues, including divorce, fostering, first love and how it feels to be the "odd one out".' *Material Matters* about STICK

'. . . sharply observed teenage behaviour, with a stimulating variety of thoughtfully drawn characters.' *Books for Keeps* about JUST HOW FAR?

LOVE'S A PAIN

A PAIN

Barbara Jacobs

CORGI
f REEWAY

LOVE'S A PAIN

A CORGI FREEWAY BOOK 0 552 525820

First publication in Great Britain

PRINTING HISTORY
Corgi Freeway edition published 1990

This book is set in 11/12pt Palatino by
Kestrel Data, Exeter

Corgi Freeway Books are published by Transworld Publishers Ltd.,
61-63 Uxbridge Road, Ealing, London W5 5SA, in Australia by
Transworld Publishers (Australia) Pty. Ltd., 15-23 Helles Avenue,
Moorebank, NSW 2170, and in New Zealand by Transworld
Publishers (N.Z.) Ltd., Cnr. Moselle and Waipareira Avenues,
Henderson, Auckland.

Printed in Great Britain by
BPCC Hazell Books
Aylesbury, Bucks, England
Member of BPCC Ltd

Leanne Cunniffe

ACKNOWLEDGEMENTS

The Publishers gratefully acknowledge permission to reprint the following stories:

'Hens' and 'Seeing, Believing' which were first printed in *Mizz* magazine;

'The Present', 'Cat's Eyes', 'Waiting for a Train', 'Snap', 'Saturday Morning Launderette Girl', 'Mirror, Mirror', 'The Other Half' and 'Inside' which were first printed in *Just Seventeen* magazine.

Some of these stories were originally published under different titles.

The Publishers also thank D. C. Thomson & Co. Ltd for permission to reprint 'Hide and Seek' which was first printed in *Blue Jeans* magazine, and 'Fancy Me' which was first printed in *Patches* magazine.

CONTENTS

Love's a Pain

I thought Jen would get over it. We all did. After all, we'd all fallen in love and been let down. It was no big deal; well, not after you'd cried yourself to a standstill and contemplated going into a nunnery. Or, preferably, a monastery.

But I couldn't convince Jen of any of that. She was impervious even to the funnies, which was very strange because before Ashley Lyon trudged into her life with his pigeon-toed brogues and his evil ways, she'd been funnier than any of us. And weird.

Jen was always a real oddity. That's how we'd become friends, because I'm always on the lookout for anything freaky or unacceptable, and she was both, back in the First Year. She wore glasses with no glass in them, stick-on tattoos which everyone thought were real, earrings made out of ring-pulls, and an assortment of junky slides and bits of fabric and beads in her hair. She was always being sent home from school for looking outrageous, which I thought was brilliant because my rebellion and humour were verbal, not visual, and earned me detentions instead of impressive little notes to take home to my parents.

In Jen's case there was only one. Parent, that is. Later on, over the Ashley Lyon affair, Ellie, who was always in training to be an agony aunt with a no-nonsense bosom and square shoulders for crying on, said that Jen's mum was basically the problem because she hadn't grown up either, and she had a point, because Jen said that when she took the notes home her mum smoked them.

Actually, I didn't believe her. Ever. Even though Jen's mum was stuck somewhere in a late sixties' time-warp, and her background wasn't as conventional as mine, for instance, or Ellie's, or Mo's, it wasn't as wild as she made out. As a comedienne myself, although not quite an actress in the Jen class, I've always understood the importance of a little exaggeration to get a joke across. In fact, if I were to become boringly philosophical at this point, I'd say that all there is to humour is tasteful embellishment of the nasty truth. But I'm not being philosophical, so I'll say that most of the time Jen was putting one over on most of us, and that's what made us laugh.

And I honestly thought she was still joking when she told me, just after we'd finished our exams, that she'd fallen in love with Ashley. I actually laughed. Then she got these two big tears in her eyes so I shut up, but warily, just in case she was going to say, 'Made you wonder then, didn't I!'

But she didn't.

In the two weeks that the romance lasted, a dreadful change came over her. She turned from a genuine weirdo with a genuine chip on her shoulder into something that looked as if it had stepped from the pages of an American teen romance. The jerkin she'd worn for as long as any of us could remember, the one with the appliquéd whale on the back and the badges on the front, disappeared mysteriously. That jerkin *was* Jen. The bits and pieces she'd added to it and cut from it over the years, the patchwork and embroidery, the obscene or threatening, funny or tragic messages of the badges, all spelt out a view of life which was as rich and persuasive as the girl herself.

'Where's your coat, Jen?' I asked her on the night of Mo's party.

'Oh . . . er . . . flushed with its own success. I drowned it down the loo,' she smirked. 'Have you met Ashley?'

'Him? I've known him all my life,' I snarled, shaking hands with him. He had hands like cold fried haddock. 'Still training to be a plonker, Ashley?'

'I'm in insurance,' he said, frowning because he didn't quite understand.

I raised my eyebrows at Jen. She didn't raise them back. That's when I realized that something extremely serious had happened to her. It was obvious that she hadn't lost her sense of humour completely, only as far as Ashley was concerned. She couldn't see beyond his broad shoulders and blond hair and blue eyes.

'What're you lumbering yourself with *him* for?' I hissed to her as soon as he drifted away for drinks.

'He's different,' she said.

'He's not different!' I yelled. 'He's a clone. Come on, Jen! There's millions of idiots looking like him working in the offices all down Lever Street.'

'Yeah, but he's different from *me*, isn't he?' she asked.

Maybe she had a point. Once. Not any more. Not in the squeaky clean face with its Princess Di eye-makeup, or the slide-free hairdo, or the pale blue frock.

'Are you just, you know, playing at this?' I whispered, conspiratorially.

'No,' she said, looking me straight in the face. 'I'm in love.'

I thought that was the punch-line, so I almost laughed. But Jen just continued to look at me, her level gaze challenging me to make another wise-crack. I couldn't. I just left her to it and sat in the blare of music and the rattle of conversation, watching her pale face bobbing at the level of Ashley's shoulder. For a girl in love she looked as if it wasn't exactly a belly laugh.

'I'm worried about Jen,' Ellie murmured, sidling up to me.

'You and me both,' I agreed. 'I mean, Ashley Insurance of all people!'

'It's worse than that. She says she's in love,' Ellie groaned.

'Oh,' I giggled. 'She told *you* that story too, did she?'

'Mind if I ask . . . . ? How did you feel when you went out with Ben? And Mick?' she persisted.

'Used,' I spat.

'No, seriously. When you thought you were in love. How did it feel?' Ellie asked, in that serious psychoanalytic manner of hers.

I wriggled. I didn't, and still don't, enjoy Ellie's emotional quarrying. Soul-bearing isn't my thing.

'OK,' I mumbled.

'Good OK, or iffy OK?' Ellie pursued.

'Good OK, I suppose.'

'And very good, at times?'

'Mmm. Yeah,' I blushed.

'Me, too,' Ellie sighed. 'And I just asked Mo how she felt about Justin, and it's the same – you know, pretty good. Like love seems to be a very positive feeling.'

'If you don't count the negative bits,' I agreed, reluctantly.

Ellie ignored me. She was doing her famous puckered-forehead look.

'But you see, Jen's taking it very differently. Know what she just told me? She says she knows she's in love because she feels so awful,' she said.

'Huh?'

'Ill. She feels ill all the time. Sick and stomach-churning. She says she's done a lot of reading about love, and that's what you're supposed to feel like. She said all the great poets felt ill when they loved someone.'

'Oh hell!' I stammered. 'I must be in love with Ashley Plonker, too, because he makes me feel sick just to look at him.'

'Take this seriously,' Ellie snapped.

'How can I? It's obviously one of Jen's jokes.'

Ellie shook her head.

'Fancy having to look at poems to find out whether you're in love or not! It's her mother I blame it on. You should be able to talk to your mother about things like this . . .'

Ellie wandered off, chuntering under her breath about the responsibilities of irresponsible single parents, while I stood grinning. I knew that this had to be a shaggy-dog story – a long and apparently pointless joke which would eventually have a very funny, Jen-like ending.

But it didn't. The only ending it had was the one Ashley gave it, when he fell for a girl he'd helped while she was struggling to get a cello on to a number seventy-three bus. Jen was devastated. If she'd believed in the malefic powers of love before Ashley left her, now she became inconsolable. I stopped waiting for the twist ending. This story just wasn't written to be funny, and I'd run out of patience with my old best mate.

'She'll be OK in time for the holiday,' Ellie said, with more hope than conviction.

We'd almost forgotten about the holiday in the light of Jen's transformation, but when Ellie reminded us it seemed like the last straw.

The holiday had been arranged in the old happy days before the exams, a mad splurge-out on a Cornish fisherman's cottage. With our holiday-job earnings, Jen's part-time income from selling earrings, and our profits from selling our GCSE cramming books to some worried fourth years, it was going to be the holiday to beat all holidays, the final wild fling before our results brought us back to reality. Now I didn't want to go. It was all ruined. Jen was playing her Mrs Rochester part, all groans, feeling sick and rejected, being pale and ill and, according to her, therefore desperately in love, so who wanted to spend a wacky week in St Ives with that? It would be like spending a week in traction.

So Jen's apologetic phone call came like a message from the gods. I tried to control my face. I knew that sympathy was what was required but I'd doled so much out that I was empty. The corners of my mouth kept lifting of their own accord as I spoke, and I knew that even though I was smiling only into the telephone, that smile would sneak into my voice in just a moment and betray me as my best friend's enemy.

'Jen,' I interrupted, finally. 'Don't rush into a decision now, not when you're feeling like this. Listen, I've got to go now. The dog just got the budgie. But I'll ring later, and we'll talk some more. OK?'

14

The grin widened as I replaced the receiver on the rest, and then I jumped up and down like a demented vulture, whooping and swinging my arms in delight before finally coming back to land and dialling Mo's number.

'Guess what?' I shrieked, as soon as Mo answered.

'Brian Watson asked you out?' Mo suggested.

'Better than that!'

'Brian Watson asked you to ask me to go out with him?' Mo asked, very hopefully.

'Oh yeah?' I sneered. 'Try again. Delete Brian Watson. Think holidays. Think Jen.'

'Do I *have* to?' Mo groaned. 'Um . . . let's see . . . She finally snapped out of it. Out of lerv.'

'If only . . .' I sighed.

'So what else would make the holiday bearable?' Mo asked.

'She's pulling out!' I yelled. 'Not coming! Leaving us to it! Apparently, the broken heart won't heal, the stomach continues to churn with unbridled passion and unrequited lerv, and she's decided to do her martyr act. She says could we possibly manage without her because she'd only be a wet blanket, so . . .' I mimicked.

'Honest?' Mo shrieked.

'Honest. She just phoned me.'

'And did you tell Ellie?'

'Give us a chance! I selected you to be the first to hear the glad tidings. I'm just nipping round to Ellie's now,' I laughed.

'Hang on. Wait for me,' Mo pleaded. 'I want to be there to see Ellie's face when you tell her. It's what we've all been hoping for, secretly, isn't it? I'm coming round. We'll go to Ellie's together.'

So, twenty minutes later, we burst in on Ellie,

dancing round like silly schoolkids just let out of detention.

Which we were. And which Ellie didn't hesitate to remind us of.

'So? What d'you think?' I asked her when Mo and I had finished doing our silly conga round the living-room.

'I think it's great news!' she giggled. 'Except . . .'

Her face fell slowly until all her features pointed downwards.

'. . . except that it's a terrible way to treat a friend,' she said, all seriously holy. Ellie knew exactly how to pierce spontaneous happiness with some very sharp guilt. 'We ought to be helping her out of this instead of celebrating the fact that we don't have to bother. We've got to put her back on the right track. We've got to save her from herself. We must. We owe it . . .'

Then she paused, and sighed.

'OK,' she said. 'I'd better be honest about this. The bottom line is that unless Jen comes, we just can't afford the holiday. Well, I can't, anyway.'

She took a notebook and pencil from the desk in the corner and quickly wrote on it the holiday costs: the rental of the cottage, the train and taxi fares, the food kitty. She wrote it all down and divided it by four with the assurance of someone who'd done this particular calculation over and over again.

'As per original costing,' she murmured, underlining the massive three-figure sum twice.

'Now look at this,' she said, taking the original total, subtracting Jen's train fare and food costs, then dividing by three. She underlined this number twice and then worked out the difference that Jen's absence would make.

'Forty-seven pounds, sixty-three pence,' she announced. 'That's how much it would cost to leave Jen out.'

'That would leave me just over two pounds' spending money,' Mo blinked.

'You've done that calculation before,' I snarled at Ellie.

'Not done it, but thought it. Haven't we all? Haven't we all wondered if we could afford to make this a threesome?' she asked.

'No,' I confessed. 'The thought never entered my head. I just thought Jen'd get over it in time for Wednesday.'

'But she hasn't,' Mo wailed.

'So now it's up to you, Tessa,' Ellie pronounced.

'Me?' I squealed.

'You're her very best friend,' Mo said.

'And you're the one whose faith never faltered,' Ellie went on. 'You believed that she'd recover in time for the holiday, didn't you? So you can help her to recover. I think we're pretty unanimous that forty-seven pounds and sixty-three pence is out of the question at this late stage? So, Tessa, off you go and persuade Jen that we really want her to come on the holiday. And tell her that she'd better leave her broken heart at home. OK?'

'Not OK,' I grumbled.

Ellie waved the sheet of calculations at me. It was a lot of money.

'I'll try,' I said.

But I didn't relish the prospect. Quite honestly, I didn't know where to begin. The Jen who had emerged during the last three weeks or so was a creature totally unknown to me. It was as if for years I'd kept watch over an ornate and intricately designed cocoon, only to see something transparent and nondescript emerging.

I stood for ten minutes outside her house, trying to talk myself into confronting her, rehearsing the different approaches I could make and failing each time. Finally, the milkman rang the doorbell and Jen's mum caught sight of me hovering on the pavement, muttering various incantations to myself.

'Tessa!' she called. 'How lovely to see you!'

That was typical of Jen's mum. She was so naturally open, even if she was a bit airy-fairy, that I immediately felt guilty for neglecting Jen for the last few weeks.

'You've come to see Jen, of course,' she smiled, squeezing my hand when I shuffled up to be let in. 'Try to cheer her up, Tessa. Mind you, I think it's a lost cause. She's discovered what I've been telling her for years. Love hurts. Roy Orbison was right. Men!' she hissed in a despairingly gentle way. 'They should all be hung out to dry and made to suffer as we suffer, shouldn't they? No-one knows what it's like to be a woman. It's a tragic legacy we hand down from generation to generation.'

I'd never really understood Jen's mum, but I'd reached the conclusion some time ago that she didn't always make a lot of sense. She was harmless enough, sort of plump and homely at heart but squashed into ethnic layered clothes. She made pots and had very spacey eyes like pale blue marbles. She and Jen appeared to live quite separate but concentric lives within the jumbled house with its liver-coloured walls and bright peeling posters. A Joni Mitchell album wailed from the kitchen where Jen's mum was obviously making more of her flower-shaped pottery which sold to all the gift shops in town.

'Did you ever see this boy who broke Jen's heart?' she whispered to me as I began to climb the stairs towards Jen's half of the house.

I nodded.

'Why?' I asked. 'Didn't you?'

She shook her head.

'I suppose he was totally unsuitable?' she asked.

'Totally,' I said.

She smiled, almost to herself, and seemed very satisfied with the answer. She obviously hadn't realized that what I meant by 'unsuitable' could be very different from what she hoped I meant. She meant James Dean.

Jen was sitting in bed, in semi-darkness, reading a magazine.

'Hi, Tessa,' she whispered. 'Have a lovely holiday without me, won't you?'

'Stop it!' I said.

'What?'

'Stop the dramatics. We've all had it up to here. Even Ellie was saying today how phoney you're getting.'

'Phoney?' Jen gasped. I knew that would bring her to her senses.

'Well, just look at you!' I insisted.

I marched across to the curtains and pulled them open so that clear sunlight flooded the room. Then I turned off the light.

'You're posing. Lying in bed, pretending to be sick, Jen. This just isn't on. What if we all did it?' I shouted.

'Did what?'

'Got sick and pale and useless every time we fell in love. Just think. How many women are there in the world? And how many fall in love? Ninety per cent? Most of the world's female population would be flat out and useless ninety per cent of the time. Only little kids and toothless grannies would function like human beings.'

'Stop being statistical,' Jen complained. 'You sound like Ellie.'

'Yeah, well, Ellie's angry with you. Mo's angry with you, and I'm angry with you!' I yelled. 'You're ruining the holiday.'

'I . . . I don't mean to . . .' Jen stammered. 'It's just that I feel so awful every time I think of him. That's the way my mum feels about my dad. The first time I was out with Ashley, my stomach turned over and over. It's gone on doing that ever since, every time I even think of him. And look . . .'

She thrust this dreadful gushy romantic magazine under my nose.

'Read that bit!' she instructed, poking at the text with a well-bitten fingernail.

'Amber,' said the slush, 'gazed deeply into Sir Tarquin's eyes. She felt a stab of anguish more painful than any dagger. Her heart turned over like a sick bird. She knew this feeling, this pain. She knew the terrifying power of love. Sick inside, she trembled and threw herself on his neck . . .'

'Crap,' I said.

'And that's your considered critical opinion, is it?' she sneered.

'That's more like you, Jen!' I grinned. 'That's what we miss, all of us. The holiday wouldn't be the same without you. You've got to come. And you've got to behave.'

'Meaning?'

'Drop the love's-a-pain act. This is going to be a laugh, this holiday. We're going to have fun. Remember what that was like? And we're going to

20

find you someone who's far more unsuitable even than Ashley,' I grinned.

'Promises promises!' she grimaced.

'I'll call for you Wednesday morning, seven o'clock,' I said. 'And Jen . . . why don't you start making yourself a new waistcoat? It'll make you feel better.'

'Something has to,' she groaned.

'You said it!' I laughed.

I felt very proud of myself. I'd never thought of myself as having a natural talent for medicine or psychiatry, salespersonship or dictatorship. But I flattered myself that I'd brought Jen back from the brink of a fatal love attack to something approaching the living dead.

'She doesn't look as if she's completely over it,' Mo said, in a fine turn of understatement as we all rattled down to Cornwall in the train.

Jen was corpse-pale, with puffy eyes and a tight smile that winced every so often. She didn't say much. Most of the time she stared out of the window, and I knew she was finding it difficult to break out of her tragic act, because her eyes were far away and her mind was obviously clicking up Ashley's name and his expressionless little face.

'It'll take a day or two,' I whispered back. 'Once she's got the sun on her face and the wind in her hair . . .'

'And food in her stomach,' Ellie sniffed in her practical way, staring pointedly at the salad-on-brown sandwich with one bite out of its corner which sat on the table in front of Jen.

But the cottage brought a real smile to Jen's face. It was a perfect whitewashed cottage, only a cobbled street away from the beach and harbour.

Windowboxes of brilliant geraniums and dark blue trailing lobelia, and bright yellow gingham curtains, completed the picture of ye perfecte holiday cottage.

Inside was just as charming. The tiny bedrooms had sloping ceilings and exposed beams, patchwork quilts and views over miles of blue sea. Downstairs, the through lounge/kitchen had patio doors at the back leading to a walled courtyard filled with tubs of lavender and roses, stocks and flowering thyme. The warm sun-trap garden was heady with fragrances. Jen sank on to one of the sun-loungers.

'Beautiful,' she murmured, smiling.

Mo and Ellie and I smiled too. It was the first real smile we'd seen for ages. We set to work unpacking, turning on the fridge and immersion heater, and making beds. Mo and Ellie were to share the larger bedroom, Jen and I the smaller one. Then Ellie and Mo went out to shop while I set the table in the courtyard. Jen had disappeared.

I wasn't really resentful. I knew that Jen hadn't got the same domestic graces as the rest of us, but it was fairly selfish of her to camp out in the bathroom while we all set to with the Mrs Mop impressions. But when she appeared smiling, with her sewing, and apologized for being lazy, she disarmed all of us. She was obviously trying as hard as she could to be normal.

Mo wanted to go out later, but Jen persuaded us that a walk round the town, just to explore, might be the best idea as it was getting late. So that's what we did. We were back and in bed by ten, exhausted after the long journey.

It was very dark when I heard Jen's voice calling my name. For a while I couldn't orientate myself. Streetlamps and car headlights took the black out of the darkness at home, turning my room at night to a sulphurous twilight, but here there were no edges to the night.

'Tessa,' Jen's voice called.

It came from a long way away. Even when I'd decided where I was and why, and where the other bed was, I couldn't locate Jen. Then, as my eyes adjusted to the light, I saw that the bedroom door was open and that Jen was coming out of the bathroom opposite. She looked like death. I'd never seen anyone look so ill.

'Tessa,' she murmured. 'I'm sorry. I've been trying really hard, but I just had a dream about Ashley and I feel awful again.'

She half stumbled towards me and I almost pushed her into her bed.

'Is that all!' I hissed.

'Really awful,' she said, clutching my hand.

Her hand was clammy. For some reason, reflex I suppose, I placed my other hand on her forehead. It was hot.

'See?' she asked, sensing that my disbelief was ebbing. 'This is how it's been, but it's worse than ever tonight. Like I said, it's love. It's doing terrible things to me. I must be extra-sensitive or something, eh? Like my mum.'

'And Amber,' I said.

'Who?' she asked.

'The one who had a sick bird for a heart,' I reminded her, trying to be flippant to disguise my panic.

Then I went to wake Ellie, and sent her to find the telephone and an ambulance. In the early hours of the morning Jen was operated on for an appendicitis which had been grumbling for a few weeks, the doctor said. Jen looked wonderful when

23

she came round, all rosy-cheeked with sparkling eyes and a new zest for life.

'You ruined the holiday,' Mo said, the soul of tact.

But actually, it wasn't ruined for me, because I bumped into this very pleasant hospital porter who turned into a surfer on his days off.

Jen's mum came to see her. Ashley Lyon drove her down because the relationship with the cellist had ended. Jen's mum kept looking at him as if he was an alien which, in his twill trousers and polo shirt he was, to all of us.

'Don't let him come again,' Jen whispered after the first rather turgid visiting hour.

'Why? Does he make you feel bad? Sick? Ill? Stabbed with anguish?' I smirked.

'Shut up,' she said. 'He's a plonker.'

'He calls himself an insurance salesman,' I reminded her.

She paused in the middle of converting her hair into tiny Rasta plaits.

'I suppose he taught me a really valuable lesson, though. Something that'll stand me in good stead all through my life, something that is a secret shared by only a handful of those of us who've been right to the edge and back,' she mused.

'Yeah? What secret?' I asked.

'Love,' she whispered, conspiratorially, 'is a burst appendix.'

The Present

It was a soft night. A night with trailing pink ribbons of clouds in the sky, and a warm dampness in the air that settled in your hair like jewels. I dreamed, standing by the open back door, watching the road recede into mist and the cliffs stretching into darkness, just wishing the time away until eight o'clock. Then Dad would tramp into the kitchen, hitch his trousers up and tighten his belt.

'I'll be going to Rooney's,' he'd say.

Every night at eight o'clock exactly, as the chime of the clock broke into the ticking, it was the same. I could count on it. And five minutes later, as innocently as I could, I'd tell Mary that I'd be walking into the village for an hour.

And Micko would be waiting for me by the wall behind O'Mara's.

Micko filled my head like sea mist. He was tall and blond, not dark and rough, nor carroty and freckled like the other boys in town, but clear-skinned and tanned with those pale green-blue eyes, like the ocean sometimes when the sun shines over the bay at Inch.

Gossip said his grandad was American, passing through after the war, and that his grandmother, like his ma, was no better than she should have been – whatever that means. Katy Maloney once said that

Micko looked just like this famous American film star, and the next day someone said in the post office, 'Remember that famous American film star who was in the army during the war? He must've come down here, because I've heard he's Micko Brady's grandad.' In no time everyone was saying, as if it was gospel truth, that Micko Brady's grandfather was a film star.

That's how stories start round here. From nothing. They take a lie here, a thought there, a suspicion or a rumour from out of the whispers, and mix it up into evil. But, like I told Micko that first night we got together, I never believe anything I've not seen for myself, or asked about for myself. I told him I didn't believe a word of the stories about him that they spat from mouth to mouth. No, I didn't. I believed his eyes. And I believed his mouth, for how could a mouth so soft and warm lie and cheat as they'd said it had? I believed his touch, too.

I shivered, remembering that touch, and Mary looked up from the pots in the sink, and snapped, 'Come away from the door, Aisling, and then close it behind you. And stop your dreaming, girl! It's the drying-up you're supposed to be doing, not trying out your new best shirt to see whether it's waterproof.'

'Sshh . . .' I said, flapping my hand at her. 'Just a minute . . .'

Because at that very moment, the bus to Cork stopped at the end of the village street, and a girl climbed out.

It was something worth noticing, that was. The bus to Cork, at five minutes to eight, never stopped in our village, because who would be wanting to travel all the way to town at that time of night when there was no bus to bring them back?

26

And there never was a passenger like her, either. She was pale, so pale that her skin glowed coldly in the dusk, and she was wrapped in a pale, cold, green headscarf and an old tied-up mac. In her arms she carried a white, still bundle.

I watched her move, light on darkness, like some ghost or spirit. In the mist she appeared to hover inches above the ground, a trick of the damp half-light, like the ghosts I'd seen when I'd hidden with Micko in the shadows of the fuschia hedges by the cliffs. She seemed to glide and make no sound. Then there was sound: the click and bang of doors closing as she passed by. But she looked straight ahead, her eyes fixed, staring.

I wrapped my hands round my cold arms and rubbed, to fight off the goose pimples.

'Now, Aisling! Not tomorrow or the next day! It's now I'm needing you!' Mary shouted, striding across the kitchen to take my arm. Her eyes flickered towards the street to see what was taking my attention. As she saw what I saw, her body stiffened. One hand on the door, one hand on my elbow, she pulled me in and closed the door on the vision quickly, as if closing it on the devil himself. And then she crossed herself.

'Who is she? What's she doing here?' I asked.

'You're not to know. Too young to know. And isn't it you, Saint Aisling, who talks about the gossip in this village and says it's a mortal sin to spread the stories? Well, I won't be committing any mortal sin by keeping my mouth shut then, will I? Dry the dishes.'

Dad came in just then to take his coat and make his announcement, so I couldn't argue with her. Then the door slammed behind him and the clock ticked away the minutes, and I forgot all about the girl in my hurry to get out, to escape from the clock and the prison of time and duties. The way out was clear.

'I'll just be taking a walk, Mary. I'll maybe call in on Katy Maloney,' I stammered, setting down the last dried plate, holding my breath.

'A walk, is it?' Mary questioned, her head on one side, her eyebrows arched.

I'm scared of my sister. She has eyes like a night bird. They pierce right into you and suck your secrets out. But this time I prayed, 'Let her not know,' although I knew it was wrong to pray for something like that. Sometimes, though, even wrong prayers are answered.

'It's not a walk at all!' Mary laughed. 'Isn't it Katy Maloney's record collection, and those stupid love stories her mother lets her buy? Isn't that what you're in such a dither about?' she asked, confident that she knew where and why I was going.

'It might be,' I stammered, relieved, swallowing to relieve the dryness of my throat.

'Sure, it can do no real harm, I suppose! Off with you, then. And home at nine. And don't say a word to Dad about me letting you go to read that rubbish!' she sighed.

'Not a word!' I grinned, kissing her quickly on the cheek by way of a thank you, and then regretting it when I saw her eyes cloud again, and her hand rub off the kiss.

In the dark of the hall I crossed myself, giving thanks for protection again. Micko told me that crossing and praying was all superstition and that I shouldn't let myself go the way of other girls, like dried-up Mary and poor Katy who was still such a child. He said I was different. Special, he said.

Special. I glanced at myself in the grey scrap of

mirror stuck above the table in the hall. My mouth was too wide, my nose too snub, my hair too unruly. But in my new rose-coloured shirt and with just a touch of the lipstick I kept hidden in the bottom of my schoolbag, perhaps I could believe, for Micko's sake, that I was a little special.

I slipped out of the house, into the half-dark, past Rooney's – all light and music spilling out on to the pavement – up the hill, running now, left at the top by the school, round to O'Mara's and the high wall behind the pig sheds at the back. I leaned against the cold stone, panting, watching through the mist for Micko's shock of blond hair, wiping my muddy shoes on the tufts of wet grass so that I'd look my best for him, trying to slow my thumping heart so that I wouldn't show myself up by panting all over him. But my heart pounded, all the same, and my blood roared and pummelled its way through my veins, and my breath screamed in my lungs louder than the music in Rooney's bar, too loud for safety.

Pictures shaped themselves and dissolved in my mind. Micko. The fires of hell. A ghost shaped like a girl with a white bundle in its arms. Ribbons in the sky, pink like my new shirt. Mary's eyes, bright and threatening like a bird of prey. Memories safer forgotten and never, never confessed, because how could I say that I'd sinned when Micko said there was no sin?

Words buzzed and jostled in my head.

'You're late!'

'And where were you last night, Aisling Flynn, when you said you were coming to listen to my U2 tapes?'

'I was in the shadow of the fuschia hedge. That's where I was, Katy Maloney,' I imagined myself laughing back at her. 'Oh, and Micko Brady was with me, holding me tight so the ghosties wouldn't get me.'

But imagining saying it didn't make me laugh. It made me frightened, more than I'd been that night last week. But Micko said it would be all right. He said everything would take care of itself.

I told myself that as I waited, but it didn't help. The night settled round me. The cold and damp seeped under my skin like guilt. Things scuttled through the grass and dark wings fluttered too close to my face. I stood and shivered and peered through the darkness, growing colder and colder, like that pale cold girl from the bus, my skin like hers, clammy and iridescent. I heard the O'Maras' back door creak open, and from inside, from the lighted house, a clock striking nine.

I knew then that Micko wasn't coming.

I didn't cry. Not then. And I didn't cry as I ran home, making a detour round past Katy's house so that it would look as if I'd come from there. But in the night, in the tent of bedclothes, I cried and cried until morning came.

I'd believed, you see. I'd believed all those promises made in the shadows. And I'd been so proud of believing, as if that act of faith alone raised me up and above any possibility of being wrong.

The next morning there was too much giggling as I approached the bus-stop. More than usual, I mean, because there was always giggling and stupidity, silly childish jokes, and whispers about who liked whom. It was too much for my mood. I carried my schoolbag in my arms in front of me like a stiff, still bundle, and drifted towards the hysterical schoolkids with the sad certainty that I didn't belong to their world, no matter what they thought, no matter what my age. I'd seen visions and dreamed dreams. I'd cried tears like blood. For a few short secret weeks, someone had loved me. Now I was, for want of a better word, special.

'Hey, Aisling!' Katy Maloney shouted from the knot of sniggering girls. 'Have you heard?'

'Heard what?' I sighed. No doubt another vile concoction of evil chat about someone or something. Nothing important.

'About the girl who came in on the bus last night,' Helen O'Grady whispered.

'And left a present on Micko Brady's doorstep,' Anne Donovan spluttered.

'A baby. She dumped a baby on Micko Brady's doorstep, cool as you please, and then just went walking on to Cork, down the cliff path. And don't look at me like that, Aisling Flynn! Didn't I see the child with me own eyes? And didn't it cry and cry until Micko went to see and almost fell over it?' Katy breathed, triumphantly. 'It's the God's honest truth, so it is!'

In my mind's eye, I saw that girl again, drifting like a trick of the light, pale against the pink ribbon sky, holding the baby in her arms.

I knew it was true.

I knew that she'd placed the bundle on Micko Brady's doorstep, because there'd been a melancholy, a determination in the set of her lips that spoke of betrayal. I imagined that I saw her now, taking the coast path, brushing past the fuschia bushes, her arms empty. And when she turned, broken, for one last look at where she'd been, I saw that her face was my face, her tear-filled eyes were my eyes. She was part of my future.

Cat's Eyes

I felt sorry for her. You would, too, if you'd seen her struggling to get straight that first night she moved into the bedsit above mine. She was little and scrawny, with sort of see-through skin, and pale blonde hair, and big round blue eyes just clipped in at the corners. She reminded me of Boris, to tell the truth, except that Boris is fatter and quite capable of looking after himself, thank you very much.

So, anyway, I popped my head round the door, just to be neighbourly, on my way back from work, and said, 'I'm in the room below. If you need anything just shout, eh? I'm Gillian, by the way, but Gill to you. OK?'

And she put out this pin-thin hand, and said, 'I'm Catriona. I'll perhaps take you up on that offer.'

True enough, no sooner had I unpacked the shopping and put the frozen sponge out to defrost, and these pork chops that were on special offer and two days past the sell-by date anyway, and fed Boris, than she was there, standing in my doorway like a ghost. Took me by surprise, complete surprise. So I warned her about Boris. He's funny with strangers, quite protective really, more like a dog than a cat, I told her to keep her distance from him and asked her what I could do for her. Turned out she didn't have any milk or tea and wanted to know where the nearest fish-and-chip shop was, so, being me and the type of person I am, I said, 'Here, why don't you share my tea? There's enough for me and a little one!'

I'm always joking like that about my size. What I say is, if you're fat you've got to admit it before someone else tries to make a joke about it, haven't you? Get in first, I say. And it doesn't bother me, really it doesn't. She was a little scrag-end of a thing, about my age but small with it, so I didn't want her to feel overshadowed, you see. Some people do feel like that with me.

So, she stopped for her tea and told me she'd only just arrived in London, hadn't lived in a bedsit before, hadn't got a job and was really scared.

'Oh, you don't want to be!' I told her. 'Look at me. Only been here six months and just look how things're working out. I've got a nice little job in the food distribution trade . . .' I always say that. People think they can look down on you if you're on the checkouts in a supermarket, '. . . and I've got a receptionist's job lined up. I'm going places!'

Actually, the receptionist thing was only a hint. Karen, on the top floor in the one-bedroomed flat, was moving on to join her boyfriend in Australia, and she'd sort of promised me she'd put in a good word for me when she left. I've always wanted to be a receptionist. I've just never had the chances in life that some people have.

Well, Catriona looked at me with those big eyes, all envious, and my heart went out to the poor little thing, so I patted her hand and said, 'Tell you what. I'll see if I can get you a job at my place. It'd only be the first step on the ladder, mind. Probably just on cooked meats or even fruit and veg, but I'll see what I can do.'

'Would you?' she asked, all breathless.

I like helping people. Always have done. Big hips, big heart, I always say. And it was nice to have someone around I could talk to. From what she said, Karen led a pretty active social life, but apart from Weightwatchers and the pictures once every blue moon, I only had Boris.

Not that I told the girl that. Well, you don't, do you? Not when they're looking up to you to give them a helping hand. So I embroidered the truth just a little bit and told her about this Assistant Manager at work who was always pestering me to go out with him, and I made up one or two other things, like being on the committee of the social club at work and not having a minute to call my own, and, when she was going, I told her to call round any time. Any time at all.

I never thought she'd turn out to be so funny with me in the end.

The only thing I can put my finger on now, looking back, was that Boris wasn't his usual self that night. He didn't go for her legs. He didn't climb up and claw her hand. He didn't bite her, or even snarl at her. He just edged round her, his tail straight and stiff, watching, quite close to her. And I know this is a funny thing to say, but she kept staring at him, too, and she never blinked once. I remember that now.

Anyway, the next night she was on my doormat just as I was getting my key out from under it.

'Did you get me that job, Gillian?' she asked, quietly, but sort of firmly.

Tell you the truth, it'd slipped my mind to look on the staff notice board to see whether there was anything going. Well, it'd been one of those days. All this new stock had come in and it was all unmarked when it came to the till, so I had to keep ringing and asking prices. One of *those* days.

'I'm seeing Bernard, the Assistant Manager, for you tomorrow,' I told her. 'And, mind, this is a special favour. Don't really like being alone with him, if you know what I mean. Sexual chemistry, eh?'

'Right,' she smiled. 'And . . . er . . . I wondered if you'd be kind enough to get me this little list of groceries tomorrow, on your discount. You *do* get discount, don't you? There's five pounds with it. Let me know if it's any more.'

You can't say no, can you? And she was so nicely spoken. Well brought up. I could tell that. Really, it was a pleasure doing her a favour.

So I started getting her groceries. And thinking up more excuses about that job. She'd taken me so literally, see? And she had this way of looking at me – straight on, with those funny-shaped eyes that made me sweat with guilt. My heart went out to the little mite.

Just one thing, though. Boris took to sitting on her knee whenever she came up in the evenings for a piece of cake or a glass of the supermarket wine. That worried me a bit. Boris never took to strangers. Never. That's how I knew I must've mislaid things, and not been burgled. Boris would never have let a burglar get past him.

By burgled, I don't mean really burgled. Not like coming home and finding the place in ruins and having to phone the police and them doing finger-prints and identity parades and things. But just sometimes, when I came in, I got this sense that everything wasn't quite right. As if hands and eyes had been touching, looking, all round. Then there was the pillowcase Gran had crocheted an edging to. I couldn't find that. Or my egg-poacher. Or the soap dish I'd got when they were on offer. Just bits and pieces really, but it was all adding up, if you know what I mean.

I talked to Boris about it. No, I'm not stupid. I know cats can't talk or anything, but Boris was one of those cats that looked at you as if he understood, and that made you think of things you hadn't thought of before. Like, did I lose the pillowcase at the launderette? Did I give the egg-poacher to Mum when she came down to visit because, like I said to her, poached eggs aren't my favourite food? And did I throw the soap dish away with the potato peelings? Boris made me think of explanations, see?

And maybe Boris had walked on my stack of letters from Mum, and that's why they were a bit wobbly. And maybe he'd tried to open the top drawer where I kept my private things. Cats do things like that.

So I didn't really give it a second thought. Not really. Not until I came home one night and found Boris gone.

I'll remember that Thursday as long as I live. Thursdays are my late nights, so I was tired, what with collecting Catriona's groceries and diving all the way down to the staff canteen before I came home to see if there was another job bulletin up. She'd started to get really just a bit niggly about that job, and I was going to have to shut her up somehow.

Well, I walked in, and no Boris. I shouted for him. I looked everywhere – under the bed, in the wardrobe, everywhere – and then I put his food down and banged his saucer and . . . nothing. I knew he couldn't get out. All the windows were closed, and everything. But you still don't think straight when you're in a tizz, do you? So I went diving out on to the landing and crashed into Karen, who was coming down from her flat.

'Seen Boris?' I gulped, when I'd dusted her down.

She shook her head, sort of distantly.

'About that job . . .' I thought I'd remind her.

'Er, *how* many GCSEs did you get, Gill?' she asked, all cold.

'Um, five,' I said, thinking hard.

'You said seven last time,' she snapped.

'Oh, did I? Oh, well, seven, really. But I got English twice and you can't count Art, can you?' I stammered.

'Sure it wasn't just one?' she sneered, really nasty. And she'd never once been funny with me before.

I must have turned puce, because that was a bit close to the mark. In fact, it was spot on. One. Exactly one. But no-one knew about that except me and the certificate I kept in my top drawer with my private things.

'Five,' I insisted, as Karen swept down the stairs. 'And if you see Boris . . .'

'Catriona's probably got him,' she said, over her shoulder. 'She's got eight GSCEs, too, all above grade C. She showed me her certificate and her typing qualifications.'

I couldn't make out why she'd thought Catriona might have Boris. Probably because she knew that Catriona and I were best friends even if she was cleverer than me, and she'd sort of assumed I let Catriona look after him. But I didn't. Not ever. Boris was mine. No-one looked after him but me.

But I knocked at Catriona's door, just the same,

just to ask her if she'd seen him, and you could've knocked me down with a feather.

It was her room. I'd never been inside it, or even seen inside it, not since that first day. She'd been down to my place almost every night, but funnily enough she hadn't got round to asking me up. Now, as she opened the door, it looked like another world from the one I lived in. There were those peach ruched curtains at the windows, Austrian blinds they call them, and little lamps, and low tables, and a lovely print sofa, and a lace cover on the bed with this pretty crocheted-edge pillowcase and . . .

'Catriona!' I breathed.

Because there was Boris, too. Snuggling in her arms.

'Gillian,' she said. 'We were just talking about you, Boris and I. He was telling me what a lousy fat liar you are. Like he told me how you're just a checkout girl, not a trainee manager. He told me how you pretend to be better off than you are. He told me how you're not qualified to be a receptionist, and how no-one's ever fancied you, especially not this Assistant Manager you go on about. He's told me quite a lot, has Boris, over the last week or so. And I told Karen. It seemed only fair in the circumstances. And I've got the receptionist job. I start on Monday, fatso!'

I couldn't think of a single thing to say to that. Well, yes I could. Just one.

'Can . . . can I have Boris back?' I stammered, holding out my arms and blinking hard. But Boris just growled, low in his throat, and settled deeper into her arms.

'I think he prefers me,' she laughed, slamming the door in my face.

I staggered down the stairs, and sat for a long

time on my bed with my door open, just thinking, trying to think the way I could think when there was Boris to think at. But without a friend, you're lost. So it was days and days before I worked out how my cat had actually spoken to her and told her all my secrets. And then, when I did realize, I stopped leaving my key under the doormat and I got another key for my top drawer and locked Mum's letters in there with my private things.

Cats don't talk. Everyone knows that. Even the loneliest people in the world know that. Not that I'm admitting to being lonely. Cats, they just take what's offered, then see what's better, weigh it up silently, and move on up.

Fancy Me

I had to get back with that skinny Lisa. Just for the sake of having a girl around really, because they're pretty useful, girls are, if only to stop the other girls drooping themselves all over you. I reckon that a girl you're sort of used to can be better than a dog at times.

I'd missed her in a funny kind of way, after that row we'd had when I just accidentally got wrapped up in Sharon Whitehead at Kevin's party. Lisa had stormed off, and I couldn't get her to just stand there and listen to my perfectly reasonable explanation about Sharon and me reaching for the bowl of crisps at the same time and getting entangled. Girls don't listen to reasonable explanations, they just get these big wobbling tears in their eyes and go all tragic and say stupid things like 'I never want to see you again as long as I live!' End of story, according to them. But maybe I'd've liked to have written a different ending, given half a chance.

I'd been at a loose-end ever since. Not desperate or anything. You've got to be joking if you think I'd ever get desperate over a girl! I've got better things to do with my time, and anyway, there must be girls queuing up everywhere waiting for me to go out with them, if I could be bothered to go out and look. But I couldn't. Lisa was habit-forming, and no-one else I casually smiled at had her big beautiful grin, and her sparkly eyes, and her funny bouncy way of walking, and her surprising way of talking about things I liked talking about, too. And, but this is a bit personal, I'd never kissed anyone else, or even wanted to. OK – except Sharon Whitehead – but that was an accident, like I said.

So I rang Lisa up, and I told her I'd forgiven her for being stupid and said I'd see her on the touchline, watching me play football, on Sunday afternoon, but she just made a funny choked sound and slammed the phone down. And she didn't show on Sunday, even though she could've stopped me scoring that own goal if she *had* been around, grinning at me the way she used to do, with her nose all red and her eyes all bright.

And then I just happened to bump into Lisa's best friend, Julie, when she was coming out of school on Thursday. Bumping into her took quite a lot of organizing, actually. She was late, and I had to stand outside her school in the cold, freezing to death, for about half an hour before she came out. I've never liked Julie. I reckon Julie put some funny ideas in Lisa's head, the way girls' best friends always do, but Lisa wouldn't see me so I had to persuade someone to talk her round, didn't I?

'You've got a nerve, Gary Hughes!' Julie said. 'Asking me to get you back with Lisa after the way you showed her up at Kevin's! Caught in the act, weren't you? Poor Lisa's dead upset, and no wonder. You've got *no* chance!'

'Aw, go on. Do something, can't you? Ask her to let me off this once!' I begged, and begging doesn't come easy to me.

'Dunno. Ian fancies her, and . . .' Julie muttered.

'Ian Henderson? That idiot? I'll kill him!' I

snarled. 'If he lays a finger on my Lisa, I'll kill him.'

'Ooh, got it bad, haven't you? Different story when it was you and Sharon getting to know each other over a bowl of crisps!' Julie sneered. And then she looked at me, the way some girls *can* look, like a relenting cobra, and said, 'She'll be at Moira's tomorrow night. There's a party on.'

'Hey, thanks, Julie!' I grinned. My subtle magnetism had worked, even on a snake in the grass like Julie. I added a wink to the grin.

'Slight problem. It's fancy dress,' she said, grinning back, all superior.

My heart plummeted. Fancy dress! Where was I going to get a Batman costume in twenty-four hours?

'Tell you what though, since it's you, and I've always had a soft spot for you – my big brother can't go. He has to go to London on duty, and he's hired a costume. You could borrow that, if it helps!' she smiled.

I hugged her. It was like hugging a barbed-wire fence, but still, you have to do these things. 'You're a pal!' I said, giving her my wink again – the atomic one.

'I'll send it round!' she said. 'And wipe that one-eyed look off your face.'

Never trust a barbed-wire fence, or a girl's best friend, that's what I say.

Friday, I was bubbling inside all day. I was determined I'd do Lisa proud. I even bought a little present for her, a pair of earrings I'd seen in a shop the day after she walked out on me. I felt a bit of an idiot buying a present for her. I'd never done that before, but she'd got to me, so I pushed the boat out for once.

I had a bath, and another shave, just to make sure I was kissable round the jaw-line, and I splashed smelly-stuff all over me, and then I opened the box with the costume in, the one Julie had left with Mum, and for a moment I nearly gave up.

It was a rabbit costume. I'm not joking. A white rabbit. Well, you can imagine! I threw it across my bedroom, and the box after it, then sat on the bed and said, 'No way!' And then I came round. I mean, Julie's brother was going to wear it, wasn't he? And he's six foot three, sixteen stone, and a policeman. So I talked myself into it, for Lisa's sake. It wasn't *too* bad. I just had this problem with the ears flopping, and paws take some getting used to, and there was a carrot with the costume, to hold I suppose, but I drew the line at a two-foot carrot. A rabbit costume is stupid, but carrots are uncool. And I'm generally thought of as being dudey. Slightly moderately dudey.

I had to go to Moira's in a taxi. After the effect of the costume on Mum, uncontrollable hysterics is a nice way of putting it, I didn't have the nerve to go on the bus, because bus-drivers are all trained comedians these days. Taxi-drivers, too, I discovered. That bloke didn't stop wisecracking all the way, and he nearly drove into a lorry laughing at one of his jokes about my fluffy tail and powder puffs . . .

But I got there in one piece. I was all wound up, with one thing and another: the funny feelings about seeing Lisa again, the strain of holding myself back from knocking that taxi-driver's teeth into his meter with one neat rabbit punch, and the woolly heat of the costume. So I was already in the front door and grabbing myself a drink, and trying to chat up the odd girl or two, for practice, before I noticed.

No-one else was in fancy dress.

And not only that, everyone was lying about the place, screaming with laughter, holding each other up, organizing conducted tours of the kitchen where I was drinking, doing no-one any harm, and then collapsing in shrieks of wild giggles. I tried to blend into the kitchen units, quietly, but it didn't work. The doorway to the kitchen was crowded with helpless girls, screeching and hooting, and Julie stood in the middle of them, pointing at me.

'Teach him to make a fool of Lisa!' she was yelling. 'Ever seen anyone look as stupid as him?'

I couldn't force a single word out. I couldn't yell. I couldn't do anything except stand there with a big ache inside, thinking about Lisa and how much I really missed her, and how much she must hate me to do this to me, and . . . and how much, maybe, I deserved it. My throat felt tight, but I knew it wasn't tears, because you don't, do you? And then I saw her – Lisa. And that was the end, really. The clincher. There was something moist and tickly running down my cheek and she looked at me funny, her head on one side, almost as if she cared . . .

'Your idea, I suppose?' she hissed at Julie. 'Well, I don't think it's very funny. How would you like it? Shown up, in front of everyone?'

'You still fancy him?' Julie stammered. 'You still fancy that?'

Lisa didn't answer her. She wasn't laughing, though.

'Hi, Gary!' she whispered, stretching out her hand to wipe my cheek, gently. My whiskers quivered. The crowd disappeared. I pulled Lisa

45

towards me and held her tightly against the idiotic white fur.

'I've missed you! I'm sorry for what happened,' I heard myself croaking.

And, for once in my life, I wasn't pretending at all. There didn't seem to be any point. Not when you're a six-foot bunny and that's how everyone will think of you for ever and ever and never stop reminding you.

All except one person.

Waiting for a Train

Jess waited.

A promisingly bright sun, only as yet half-awake, cast light and darkness, warmth and chill along the deserted country station platform. She sat on a flaking bench in a patch of sunlight, watching the rails shimmering into haze, leaves turning in the breeze on distant overhanging trees, birds foraging, grass bending silver-green on the cuttings, cow-parsley thrown like lace along the winding lanes. And she listened to the silence, and her own breathing.

The silence was comforting. As was the warmth. And yet there was something strange, not quite right, about that quiet and the occasional flurries of birds' wings and birdsong. She glanced again at her watch. Ten minutes to eight. By now, surely, someone had usually arrived. Where was the man with the briefcase and the pale macintosh and the neatly combed wisps of hair guarding a bald spot? By the time she'd parked and padlocked her bike, he was usually pacing up and down, irritably. She missed the metronome regularity of his step, his frowning morning nod in her direction and in the direction of the station-master in his shiny trousers and bell-hop jacket. Yes, where was the stationmaster? Mr Whistle, Fat Man called him, for some reason. It was supposed to be a joke.

By now, Fat Man had usually arrived, too, flushed and panting, tie askew, shaving foam dotted round his ears.

'I'm on time, Mr Whistle, eh?' he'd joke to the stationmaster, smiling untidily as well to the man with the briefcase.

'Always on time, sir. Always on time. I could set my watch by you!' the stationmaster always replied. A daily ritual. But today . . . ?

Still, Jess's watch showed the time at ten minutes to eight. Perhaps her watch was fast. Perhaps she was early. Perhaps this was what life was really like before people and trains moved into it: still, peaceful, sleepy in sunlight. But strange.

Perhaps she ought to lie back on the scarred bench, watch the leaves turn and the grass blow and the rails glimmer to a vanishing point rather than fret for time to pass, and the scene to be spoiled by noise and racing to work. It was a beautiful morning. The calm after the storm.

The storm had caught her unawares and unprepared the previous night. She had been late at school, struggling with an essay that had to be written in the library and a headache that threatened to split her skull open while clouds gathered in purple swirls outside the arched windows. There was the first flash of lightning as she stepped from the later train, and the stationmaster had warned, 'It'll break at any minute. You'll get drenched. Missed the four-fifteen from town, did you?'

'Essay to write,' she'd explained heavily, peering through the grey-blue darkness and looking at her watch. 'It's a bit early for lighting-up time. My bike lamp's not working, either.'

48

'It's only five forty-five. It's the storm coming. That's what's making it dark. Better get going, hadn't you?' he'd said.

And a few minutes from the station the heavens had opened, rain so thick and heavy, bouncing from the steaming road, that she rode blindly, desperately, drenched and terrified.

But now, this morning had brought quiet and sunlight, heat haze and the green fresh scents that damp and warmth create. So restful. Her eyelids began to droop and close.

She jolted herself awake, remembering. This was the morning she had promised herself to do more than nod shyly in the direction of the boy in the blue sweater and the crumpled jeans. Yesterday evening, copying out those endless quotations, she'd thought about him, about the glances she saw him cast sometimes in her direction while they were waiting for the eight-ten to town. His name was Robert. Fat Man had called him that. He'd shouted, the previous morning, 'Isn't it time you finished that studying, Robert, and got down to helping your mum and dad run the farm?'

'Not much call for an artist on a farm, Mr Timpson,' the boy had said, very quietly and politely, masking the fact that this was obviously a sore point. Jess had grinned at him briefly, in support, to show that she would understand if ever Robert wanted to discuss it with her. She knew all about being the odd studious one out of a family that could see no further than the acres of arable land stretching to their narrow horizons. She needed to talk about it.

Robert had said, earlier that week, 'The train's late.'

That was as much conversation as they'd ever

had. She'd replied, 'Yes. Sometimes, I wish it would never come.'

And that particular morning, that was exactly how she'd felt, wanting just to sit and watch the boy's gentle shyness turn into conversation, questioning, friendship, while the day travelled past both of them, sunrise to sunset.

This morning, though, she wanted more than just the quiet. Quiet is painful when you're stranded inside it, away from real life, waiting for a boy, or a train, or something. The quiet irritated her. It threatened to swallow her up, whole, before she'd done what she wanted to do.

Anxiously, she glanced at her watch again. Ten minutes to eight. Early morning. Sunlight. Silence.

At that exact moment, Robert looked again at the station clock ticking away the dusty minutes in the window of the waiting-room. Eight minutes past eight. Then he looked at the station entrance, and at the wooden railing edging the car-park. Her bike wasn't there. Nor was she. Not anywhere. He shivered under the grey skies. Last night's storm had changed the weather. Today it was cold and overcast, a wretched day. Rain threatened again, and his mother had forced him into a green oiled jacket that made him look like a yuppie, or a farmer's son. He felt quite ashamed, embarrassed, not himself somehow. If that girl looked at him, when she finally did arrive, and giggled, what would he say? He couldn't say, 'We've got this party at college on Saturday, and I know I don't know you very well, in fact not at all really, but I'd like you to come with me.' He couldn't say that, all dressed up like a rodent exterminator. Girls who looked like she did, almost fragile, with huge blue eyes and clouds of soft burnt umber hair, didn't accept invitations from boys in waxed jackets, did they? Especially from boys they'd never really spoken to.

But he would never know, unless she appeared. And until, and unless, she appeared, he would have to hide inside the green tent for warmth. Perhaps he would whisk it off, throw it down at her feet across one of the platform puddles, invite her to walk on it, and on his dreams, if she liked. Perhaps he had far too much imagination. Perhaps he lived in a dream-world, as his mother hinted often enough. But that girl could help the dreams along. She could. She was beautiful. The memory of her face tugged at him with an urgency that was out of all proportion to the tenuousness of their relationship.

The rails began to vibrate.

'On time!' Fat Man smiled smugly, gesturing towards the approaching train.

'About time!' the bald man breathed, irritably. 'Not the sort of day to be hanging about in the cold!'

The sun flickered briefly between clouds as the train approached, and the boy caught his breath. There she was! That was her, surely, on the bench at the end of the platform! Then the sun was swallowed by clouds again, and he blinked. She was gone. The shadow had dissolved.

'Looks like our little cyclist missed the train this morning, Mr Whistle!' Fat Man smirked, as Robert watched frantically for her to come wheeling into the car-park, the wind in her hair, her cheeks glowing.

'Didn't you hear, sir? I thought everyone knew. That poor kid was in an accident last night, in the storm,' the stationmaster murmured. 'I warned her.

I was the last one to see her. Off the five forty-five. And not five minutes later . . . It doesn't bear thinking about. Bike lights didn't work, lorry driver didn't see her, and . . .'

The bald man shuddered as the train pulled in. He'd quite liked that kid.

'Not . . . not . . .' he stammered, a question hovering in the intonation. 'Such a pretty little thing . . .'

'No. Not, er . . . Still alive, just about. In a coma, sir, I believe. At the County Hospital.'

'She'll pull through, though?' Fat Man asked, ignoring the train which now drew up in front of them.

The stationmaster shrugged.

'Can't tell with comas. Who knows? Who knows?' he asked philosophically, like a man who knew all about everything but wouldn't say because it was all too painful to face.

'In the County Hospital?' Robert blurted, pushing the others aside urgently.

Fat Man began to climb into the train, breathing hard. The bald man followed, shaking his head sadly.

'That's right, sir. Now, would you mind?' the stationmaster asked, gesturing with his head towards the waiting train and fixing his whistle between his lips. Even tragedies shouldn't delay his trains.

'I've got to see her. Now,' Robert decided, out loud, closing the carriage door. 'Now.'

'So you won't be taking this train?'

'No!' Robert called over his shoulder, diving through the exit towards his muddy motorbike. 'No. Not today.' He broke into a run. There was no time to lose. None at all. It was quarter-past eight almost.

By half-past, if he took the Wroxham road, he could be at the hospital. It didn't matter any longer what he would say to her, what he was wearing, what explanations he would give. It would come right, somehow.

In the sunlight, Jess waited. Sunlight and the hypnotic sound of a repeated thrush's song tugged her towards sleep, but she blinked herself awake, again and again. Today, she would definitely say something to that boy. If she fell asleep, she might miss him. How much longer? She glanced at her watch. Ten to eight. Still ten to eight. Still. Quiet. Still waiting. She would wait for him.

Snap

Janys organized the camping holiday. Typical, that was. It was typical that it should be Janys, because she was one of those girls who insisted on organizing everything from who gets off with whom, to who finishes with whom, and even providing sausages on sticks, fizzy pink wine and last year's chart sounds to accompany all this getting off and finishing with. We all tried to avoid Janys's dreadful parties, but always failed. She got very upset if we didn't go along with her plans, and her face would go all smacked-looking, so, usually, we did what she wanted.

Even camping. I mean, that was typical, too. When I said, one boring Sunday afternoon in our back garden, 'I wish I could get away from all this,' and Dil and Mo agreed with me, we were talking about needing to shake the dust of broken romances with two-timing English boys off our heels. I was thinking about Crete, I remember, because Jo Simons had just gone there. Mo said she was dreaming about Florida, and Dil mentioned Lanzarote. The Yorkshire Dales didn't even elbow their miserable way into the tiniest corner of our minds. Not mine and Mo's and Dil's, anyway. But they had obviously run riot all over Janys's, because on Monday afternoon she came stomping round with a huge grin on each of her knees – she has fleshy knees that seem to reflect whatever's going on on her face – and made an announcement.

'Our troubles are over. I've managed to book us into several campsites in the Yorkshire Dales, starting on Wednesday. Just the four of us. And don't worry about the tent, I've got one. Oh, and I've hitched us a lift in my dad's van. So all you need is a bit of canned food and a sleeping bag and your dreams have all come true.'

'Was this your dream?' Mo spat angrily at me.

'No chance. I dream in technicolour, not black and white,' I muttered. 'And there's sunshine in my dreams. And men.'

'Real men, or just pathetic creatures like Dominic Nolan?' Janys hissed. Janys had never been able to understand why I fell for that slimeball, or why I didn't seem to be able to get over the fact that he'd finished with me.

'I don't know what you've got against Dominic . . .' Mo complained.

'Well, obviously she's not got her melting little body against him, and she never will have,' Dil said sharply. Dil can be very sharp. No-one, not in their right minds, could have called Janys's body little. In fact, I'd been waiting for one of Dil's witticisms about whether we were all camping out in one of Janys's old dresses, or would that be an eight-berth instead of a four-berth tent? That's the size we're talking about when we're talking about Janys.

'It'll be great fun,' Janys said. 'We'll only have ten miles walking to do each day between campsites. We'll come home healthy and tanned.'

'Especially if it rains,' Dil grunted.

'Which it always does in the Yorkshire Dales,' I said.

'Unless there's an "x" in the month,' Mo sighed. 'Then the temperatures shoot up to the low fifties.'

'I'd never last out on a walking holiday,' I decided. 'And anyway, I have to take some photos for the college photographic exhibition. I'm going to win it this year. The boys always get the prizes. I want to prove that girls make better photographers.'

'Me, too,' Mo said. 'Forget it.'

Janys's face fell. It took on the appearance of a face which had been well smacked.

'It's to help me,' Janys muttered.

'Huh?' Mo asked.

'Lose weight,' Janys whispered.

Silence fell. This was a serious moment. Very serious indeed. In all the time we'd known Janys she'd never shown the least inclination to diet or turn into a matchstick. Fat and contented was the impression she gave, which was why we all felt quite happy to make jokes about her size.

'It's the boys. They've been worse than usual recently. They're ganging up against me just because I'm . . .'

'No, they're not,' I contradicted.

'You're taking it too personally,' Mo said.

'They're no worse than usual,' Dil grinned, reassuringly.

A fat blob of a tear began to bounce down Janys's face.

'On the other hand . . .' I said.

'We could do with a break,' Mo nodded.

'Isn't that what we've been saying all along?' Dil sighed.

So there it was. Signed, sealed and delivered. A moment of female solidarity in the face of one of our little group being sniggered at because she

57

didn't reach the boys' high standards. That was a laugh for a start. Most of the boys we knew had high standards only for others. With volcanic skin and tear-gas body-odours they dared to snigger over our friend Janys? The only passable male amongst them was Dominic, although I wasn't thinking about him. I'd promised myself that I'd use the daily torture of the ten-mile walk to break myself of my addiction to Dominic Nolan. His name wasn't even going to pass into my brain cells. Not once.

That was my resolution anyway, my way of passing the initiative test which Janys called a holiday. But none of us really wanted to go. Each of us, as we clung to the innards of Janys's dad's pet supplies delivery van, seemed locked into some deep and dark deliberation of our own.

'Isn't this going to be wonderful?' Janys kept asking, but none of us could look the others in the eye.

When we arrived at the first campsite, shaken and car-sick, the gerbil smell clinging to our clothes, only Janys looked enthusiastic. The clouds hung low like water bombs on the bleak moorland site.

Janys's dad handed over the tent.

'Sure you can handle this?' he asked her.

'What do you think?' she grinned.

Of course she could handle it. Old Janys could handle anything that wasn't boy-shaped. Her dad drove away and the tent was unpacked. Janys gave instructions which none of us could follow and, as we floundered across the Mark Four Mountain Survival Igloo with Built-In Groundsheet, the water bombs exploded and the rain fell out of the sky. We were soaked within five minutes. After twenty the tent was erected, and we were shivering inside in pools of water while Janys made promises about the meal she'd cook us once the rain stopped.

Only it didn't. Not until the next morning. Our clothes steamed, our stomachs rumbled and our hearts lay like little cold stones as we dismantled the tent and got in Janys's way while she packed it up again. And, an hour later, we were just about to leave the campsite when I saw the car.

I blinked. Then I looked again.

It was a Ford Cortina in royal purple with one orange wing and a white trim. Two hubcaps were missing. The back number plate hung off at an angle.

I blinked again. There couldn't be two cars like that, could there?

'It is *over*, isn't it, between you and You Know Who?' Mo whispered, all embarrassed.

'Is it really him?' I breathed.

'Dommie? Yeah. I thought he could maybe give us a lift,' she whispered.

'You mean, you actually asked him to come up here and join us on the holiday?' I croaked.

'Yeah,' Mo blushed. 'Well, why not? He said he was interested and he's got a car, hasn't he? And, anyway, it's all over between you two, so why shouldn't I, eh?'

Dominic leaned out of the car window. My stomach did a couple of gymnastic routines. I hated him. I loved him. I liked the way one of his ears stuck out even though the other one didn't. I liked his silly goofy smile. I even liked his T-shirt for Gawdssake. I could have eaten every mouthful of his luscious body.

'What're you doing here, Snakefeatures?' I snarled at him.

'Waiting to give you lot a lift, my love,' Dominic

smiled, as nice as pie and one hundred per cent more edible.

'Hey! It's Dom!' Dil screamed, dropping the tent which she'd volunteered to carry for the first mile.

Janys, weighted down with cooking stove and super-thick, duvet- style sleeping bag, stopped dead in her tracks.

'What's he doing?' she breathed.

'Don't ask, just be grateful,' Dil breathed. 'And if you can't, you're welcome to jog behind the car.'

'Dil – that's not very nice!' Dominic called.

He sprang from the car and ran towards Janys.

'Here,' he grinned. 'Let me help. I'll take this.' He unwound the cooking utensils and the stove from round her neck, and gently took her haversack.

'Get in the car, Chrissie. Next to me, eh?' he winked as he walked past. Then he dumped Janys's haversack in the boot, and we all threw our carrier bags and backpacks on top of it.

'I'm walking,' Janys pronounced, angrily.

A spot of rain splattered on her nose. Another dripped down her glasses.

'Not in this rain, Janys, love. Come on now. Be guided by me. Mo's just told me how you held the fort last night. It's time for you to be looked after now,' he said, very sweetly, putting his arm round her shoulder.

I gulped. This new Dominic was a bit much. I wasn't quite sure whether I could take him.

'What happened to you?' I asked as he slid Janys into the back seat.

'Perhaps I grew up and learned a thing or two about myself. Perhaps I did some things I regret. Perhaps I'd like to have a try at putting them right,' he murmured, squeezing my hand.

This was very weird. I felt very weird. I felt as

if I were starring in one of my own dreams, but hadn't quite got the words right or the feelings. If this was a dream, I didn't trust it, and I wasn't sure whether I wanted to be in it. Seated, reluctantly, next to the born-again Dominic, I curled up close to the passenger door and clicked my seatbelt resoundingly. Mo sat behind Dominic, perched on the edge of her seat, her arms folded on the back of his seat, her head on his shoulder. Dil, who was Dominic's cousin, though she rarely admitted the fact, buffed her nails and kept glancing under her eyelashes at Mo and at me, wondering, obviously, when war was going to break out. Janys sat fatly behind me, her face glum and pensive, staring out into the rain-spattered landscape.

'The AA weather forecast service said changeable,' she kept saying. 'But it doesn't look like changing.'

'Not your fault, my love. You weren't to know. You left it up to the AA and they let you down,' Dominic said in consolation.

'Don't they always?' I snarled.

'Now, now! Just because you couldn't take the pressure, Chrissie,' Mo giggled throatily, nuzzling Dom's ear. I was quite pleased to see that he leaned forward suddenly so that her head made violent contact with the car window. He winked conspiratorially at me. I blushed.

It was turning out to be a strange day. It became stranger. Dominic was unrecognizable. He was so sweet and kind to Janys that she grew whiskers and fur and began to purr contentedly. Mo looked well pleased with herself for some reason. And Dom laughed like a drain at all Dil's witticisms, even though she snapped at him. But where I'd started the day by hating Mo for assuming a right to my ex-boyfriend, by the time we'd stopped for lunch, found the campsite and erected the tent, I'd decided I hated the other two as well.

Take Dil, for a start. She thought she was really clever, coming out with her witty little comments that made Dominic laugh. Really, she was bitter and twisted. Some of the things she said were really nasty. I wondered why I'd never noticed before. And Janys. She surprised me. I'd always thought of her as fairly harmless, the way a brick wall is fairly harmless. But a brick wall's only harmless because it knows its place and stays put. Janys wasn't staying put any more. She was stepping out of line, with Dominic's encouragement.

'I agree with Janys,' he kept saying, and, 'Of course, Janys is right.'

In the end, Janys believed it herself. The tent erection became a masterpiece of bossiness. Dominic stood on the sidelines and cheered Janys on as she lost her temper with all of us, although he did find time, under cover of a passing rain cloud, to stroke my cheek when no-one was looking. He was so accommodating, so pleasant, so utterly and totally unbelievable, that I had shivers up my spine. I just knew something nasty was going to happen.

It was Dominic's suggestion that we walk to the chip-shop in this tourist trap of a Yorkshire town for our supper, rather than have Janys slaving over a hot Gaz burner. So, the five of us set out, four of us jostling and shoving to hold Dominic's hand. Yes, even Janys. Her eyes had become soulful. She looked quite good, actually. Pretty, in a large kind of way. Mo had moussed her hair – on a camping holiday! Dil kept trying to say funny things. I settled, in the end, for walking behind Dominic and looking at his sticking-out ear, which looked even more fascinating from behind than it did from in front. One half of me wanted to be rid of him once and for all. The other loved him with a fierce possessiveness.

'I'll buy your chips,' Janys announced when we arrived at the chip-shop. She unzipped her little tartan purse. I could have strangled her with the shoulder-strap. I mean, who outside of Guide sixers and people who watch *Blue Peter* have tartan purses? You can see how unreasonable I felt.

'Thanks, Janys,' Dominic cooed, giving her a little squeeze. 'And I'll go and make a short phone call, if I may.'

He pointed to the telephone box which stood outside the chip-shop. We all smiled dutifully and watched him go. Then we ordered, and waited as the Chinese owner put more chips in to fry.

The fat spluttered. A television on a bracket over the man's head squealed out a Chinese kung fu movie.

None of us spoke.

Then I did. I couldn't help it.

'I wish you'd keep your hands off my Dominic,' I hissed at Mo.

'Your Dominic?' Dil squealed. 'Since when? Don't fool yourself, Chrissie. You never did have quite the style for our Dom.'

'Or the looks,' Mo said.

'You can talk!' Janys burst in. 'Have you seen what that mousse has done to your hair now the rain's got to it?'

'Oh, listen to her. Miss Fashion Victim herself!' Dil sniggered.

'I've got as much right . . .' Janys began to say.

'You've got at least twice as much in some departments,' Mo giggled, cruelly.

63

'At least *I* haven't let myself go!' I chimed in.

'No. But Dom let you go, didn't he?' Dil purred, cattily.

There was a quick burst of oriental cymbals, a Chinese version of 'The End' flashed on to the television screen, and then there was silence. The chips were being ladled into newspaper. It was so quiet, after our row, as we all stood seething and the television hummed imperceptibly, that we could hear, quite clearly, Dominic's voice drifting from the phone box outside . . .

'No, I told you, Steve,' he was laughing. 'They're all eating out of my hand. Yes, even Hannibal's favourite elephant, old Janys Thunderthighs. Thank goodness that stupid Mo told us about the camping holiday. Anyway, the plan is to catch them unawares, tonight or in the morning. You should see them now! They're really shot at! Like drowned rats. I think I could even manage to get Janys to pose wearing nothing but a tent and a balaclava. Yes. Honest. There's no way I won't win the "Holiday" section of the photographic contest. I might even win the "Pets and Animals" section if I catch Janys in her nightshirt. Cross your fingers, anyway, Steve!'

Dominic was grinning from ear to ear as he stepped back into the chip-shop. Another kung fu film began. We grinned back at Dom, all four of us, all holding our chips and smiling banana smiles, like a well-posed photograph.

'Salt and vinegar?' Janys asked, sweetly.

'Yes, please, Janys love,' Dom smiled, stepping into our charming circle.

Janys passed the vinegar to Dil. She was the tallest, almost as tall as Dom. Height ran in the family, so it was quite easy for her to shake the vinegar into Dom's hair as Mo shook the salt cellar down the open neck of his shirt.

'Give him his chips,' Janys instructed me.

We always did what Janys said. She was a brilliant organizer. So, I pulled out the waistband of Dom's jeans and emptied the chips inside.

Dom squealed and jumped.

For a while, it was better than the kung fu movie. The Chinese chip-shop owner even smiled as Dom lurched off down the road, picking chips out of his jeans. When we arrived back at the campsite, his car had gone.

Funnily enough, it didn't rain again. The sky was clear and the sun blazed down for the rest of the week as we sauntered through the daily ten-mile stint, giggling the way mates can giggle together once they've ironed out any little niggles. Janys lost a stone. Mo lost her fear of spiders. Dil met a boy from Liverpool and lost the competition to find out who could say the nastiest thing first.

And I lost that addiction to Dominic Nolan and came back tanned and ready to love and lose all over again.

But Dominic had lost most of all. He'd lost his mystique. He never did find it again, not after we'd seen him with chips in his pants. My photo of that incident won the 'Humorous' section of the college summer photographic competition, and the overall trophy for best in the show.

Saturday Morning Launderette Girl

The girl was a mystery. And exotic with it. Once or twice a week she'd appear at the club completely alone, step out on the dance floor, do a couple of routines with the best dancer in the room, and then vanish. Every time she walked in, the boys would make room for her, then lean forward, watching her, while the girls leant back, arms folded, clucking jealously, trying to sneer. She was like the centre of some strange foreign flower, swaying like a pollen-heavy stamen, surrounded by in-curving and out-curving petals.

'Amazing!' Tony would breath every time, almost bent double over the bar, watching her. Perhaps it was her dancing. She was the best dancer I'd ever seen, even including those on the television. But I don't really think that's what he was interested in. She was beautiful.

'Huh!' I'd say, without fail, rapping my fingers on my tray, waiting for the trance to end, for customers to order drinks again, and for my boyfriend to pop his eyes back in their sockets and cast a casual glance in my direction again. But I knew that there was no way I could compete with her. So I rapped my fingers and watched Tony watching her until the anger and envy subsided. Then I'd watch her, too.

And her clothes! Mind you, she could get away with them with her almost hipless slim body, that dusky skin, and the clouds of blue-black hair. She'd appear in a kind of full-length shift in green satin, beaded and sequinned with silver at the high neckline. Or she'd be plunged into black velvet, shaped to her pencil slenderness, with the V-neckline pointing somewhere beyond her navel, her arms bangled in beaten brass, her hair tied back with flying gold ribbons.

'Sexeee!' Tony would whistle as the girl writhed and bumped and slithered, centre floor.

'Wish you felt that way about me,' I'd complain, sulkily.

'Different kind of sexy, love,' he'd grin. 'That one's got three Xs in it. You're more the domestic sexy kind, the sort of girl you'd fancy in a Saturday morning launderette, if you see what I mean. No offence. But you've got to admit . . .'

I did have to admit. But I didn't like doing it. And the waitress uniform in the club, the bow-tie, white shirt, waistcoat and wide trousers, didn't do a great deal to flatter my size-fourteen curves. Still, Tony wasn't exactly Muscle of the Month, except perhaps to me, especially when he stood behind the bar where only his sparrow chest, long thin face and skinny neck were evident, and his greatest asset, his endless legs, were hidden from sight. I liked him. He liked me, so he said. But his boggling at the incredible dancer always set up the niggling self-doubt.

'I reckon her name's Dolores,' he said to me one night, as he drove me home in his rusty Cortina with the creaking exhaust.

'Who?' I asked.

'That mystery girl. What do you reckon? Does she look like a Dolores to you?'

'Doris,' I spat.

'Nah. Doris is small and cuddly like you. And Dorises wear glasses, and have a glass of warm milk before they go to bed. With a spoonful of sugar in it. Oh, and they're over fifty.'

'And what do Dorises drink at the bar?' I asked, trying to turn his attention away from my rival and towards a game we often played – 'Who Drinks What?'

'Dorises drink sweet sherry,' he said, decisively. 'And Dolores, she drinks tequila. Only tequila! Tequila on her cornflakes, tequila sauce on her hamburgers.'

'She's never ordered a drink, ever!' I argued.

'Well, she wouldn't, would she? She knows we're fresh out of tequila. Must ask the boss to order some. Just in case she decides to chat up the bar man, eh?'

'Ohhhh!' I grinned, responding immediately, as always, to Tony's infuriatingly cheeky and irresistible smile, and nudging him in the ribs.

'Where do you think she works, where does she live, what does she do all the time she's not making your eyes stand out on stalks?' I asked him, the next time Dolores slinked into the disco and gleamed out again, dressed in a shocking-red silk and gauze harem outfit with peacock feathers in her hair and diamond-bright bells round her ankles.

'Dolores, you mean?' he asked.

'Right. Dolores. Got it in one!'

'I reckon . . .' he dreamed, 'I reckon she's . . . yeah, that's it . . . she's the daughter of this sophisticated Saudi Arabian prince. She does

69

nothing all day but eat grapes and have her toenails painted different colours . . .'

'No, she's a convent schoolgirl who slides down the drainpipe every so often with her arms full of the rare fashion designs she's created in Homecraft lessons, and she comes down here to test them out . . .' I dreamed along with him, accidentally.

'Jeannie,' he beamed, hugging me across the counter and narrowly missing the seven lager and limes he'd just placed on my tray. 'I know why I like you! It's because, deep down, despite your stroppy little ways, you're a dreamer, too.'

'Hmmm!' I argued, awkwardly. 'Taken a look at how green my eyes are, though?'

I was jealous of the girl, no doubt about that. So it had come as something of a surprise to me, to hear myself actually encouraging Tony in his stupid infatuation and his silly games. I'd really grown up far beyond them. But these things happen when you're in love.

I was thinking that over, on my day off, when I called to see my gran who lived on the other side of the city. I knew she'd ask about Tony because she used to play bingo with his aunty, and I wanted to tell her that I thought he might start taking me seriously soon, when he'd got over having schoolboy crushes on some weird lady with dusky skin and snaky hips who danced all night for him in his dreams.

But I didn't get a chance to discuss it.

'Oh, thank God you've arrived! I need another pair of hands! The washing machine just packed up on me!' Gran howled, wading in six inches of water that had flooded the kitchen and threatened to seep through to the living-room.

'Here, take these for me, love, will you? Sorry

they're sopping wet. Here, dump them in the laundry basket and take them to the launderette on Slater Street while I clear up the mess before your grandad comes home!'

And a hundredweight of grubby, soaking laundry was thrust at me, catching me in its bow-wave, drenching me from head to foot. I caught sight of myself reflected in the newsagent's glossy window as I trudged past, hair limp, skirt sodden and clinging to my generous legs like a wet flag on two flat flagpoles. A mess. No wonder Tony spent his waking hours gurgling and romancing over a girl he'd never quite met, when the girl he had met had turned out to be, as he said himself, the sort of girl you'd fancy in a Saturday morning launderette.

Dismally, I leaned on the door of the launderette until it gave under my weight and the weight of the washing, and tottered in. Despite what Tony had said, I wasn't all that familiar with the workings of the big industrial machines, grimy with clogged blue washing powder, that lined the walls. I'd never been in a launderette before. I managed to shove the washing into an empty machine and then I was lost.

'Excuse me . . .' I said to the headscarved, gum-chewing attendant, who was sitting in a small cubicle, plugged into a personal stereo and reading a magazine, 'Could you show me how the machines work?'

'Uh?' she gawped. 'Yer what?'

She didn't even release one of her ears from the stereo. From six feet away I was blasted by the squawk of Prince.

'Could you show me . . .' I started to yell, mouthing my words carefully, the way you do to a foreigner.

' 'Ere!' A crooked little woman with skin like a tree-trunk grabbed my arm. 'No use trying to get through to that one. Dead uppity she is. And some need to be! Common as muck! Let me help you, dearie, I'll soon sort you out.'

And she did, handling my machine like an expert mechanic, even adding the kick for good luck and a dab of her own special blue whitener before settling down, on the plastic chairs provided, to the cup of machine coffee I'd treated her to, and the story of her life. I'm the sort of person people always tell the story of their lives to. Usually, too, I listen hard.

This time, though, my eyes kept straying to the cubicle where the girl sat, reading slowly with a pained expression, chewing spasmodically, tapping her feet, wriggling her shoulders and giving herself the occasional relief of dragging her gum from her mouth in a long grey string before winding her tongue round it and sliding it back. There was something familiar about her . . .

The tree-trunk woman had come to the time in her story when she and her family were bombed by a doodle-bug in the Blitz, before the blinding light of recognition hit me.

'Dolores!' I gasped.

'No, Freda. Like I said. It was Freda what was buried under the rubble with only her bedroom slippers on . . .' the old lady corrected me.

But, sure as soap powder, it was Dolores, the exotic dancer from the club, now seen in her real-life role, her hair tied tightly in curling wands under the headscarf, her lithe body encased in a blotchy green-check overall, her dusky skin pallid in the cold September light.

'Well I never!' I breathed.

'Amazing, wasn't it? She just lost the one bobble from her bedroom slippers! Apart from that, all intact. Right as rain. 'Course, she had some explaining to do as to how she came to be in the back garden wearing nothing but bedroom slippers!' Tree-trunk sniffed, disapprovingly. 'Your washing's done, ducks. See? The green light's flashing!'

It was flashing with a vengeance. I could hardly wait to pile that lot up in my laundry basket, dump it in Gran's drying-out kitchen, and catch the bus back home, bursting with the low-down I'd just got about Tony's dream girl.

'Saturday morning launderette!' I'd sneer at him at the club that night. 'And forget about her eating grapes. Just gum. Strings of it. So who's a Saturday morning launderette girl now?'

It was like a delighted rumble inside me, like the start of a no-holds-barred thunderstorm, a revelation that would shatter his dreams and bring him down to reality with lightning intensity. He'd forget Dolores. He just might notice me.

But before I'd reached home, the delight in my discovery had started to weaken. And by the time I'd showered and changed for work, I knew I couldn't. I just couldn't.

'You're looking thoughtful tonight!' Tony murmured, as he dispensed four Babychams for one of my tables. 'Hey, about Dolores, I reckon she just might be Brazilian, heiress to a coffee fortune . . .'

'No . . . Indonesian. The secret daughter of a Balinese temple dancer!' I suggested, drawn in by the twinkle and excitement in his eyes, swallowing back my real-life story, inventing another happier one.

'Wow! Yes! Why didn't I think of that?' he said,

admiringly. 'Jeannie. You're one in a million. You know that?'

'Huh!' I grunted, glowing inside.

You see, you've got to let them have dreams to dream, haven't you? That's what I think. And either they grow out of them, or you grow into them. Both ways, you end up winning. Thought of the Week, that is, from a girl who knows a thing or two about Saturday morning launderettes. And love. And Dolores.

Mirror, Mirror

The door swung open, silently. I stepped inside, and my breath stopped instantly. Around the room, lining every wall, were mirrors catching sunlight, angled mirrors, twisted lumpy mirrors, that focused on the street below and filled the deserted room with reflected crowds of distorted dwarfs, gossiping, shopping, shouting, yawning, waiting in queues for buses, negotiating toy cars into tiny parking places. I'd come to find out about Phoebe and her cartoons. But here they were exactly as she drew them. Just real people in a hall of mirrors. And in the middle of the crowds, one real and breathing human girl perched at a drawing table, watching me with eyes like mirrors.

I prickled. Sticky buds of sweat tickled my spine. Scared? Me? Nick Armstrong, intrepid journalism student, finally almost in possession of the biggest story of all time . . . ?

Yes, I was scared. Scared by the mirrors, and more scared by the beauty of the girl who watched me and did not speak. She had the face of a tiny child, rounded, pink and cream, with a rosebud mouth and waterfalls of ringleted fiery hair. She looked like an Elizabethan miniature, or a wild Victorian fairy. I had never seen anyone like her. Never.

'I came to see . . . er . . . your mother. I'm Nick

Armstrong. I want to do a story on her. I know she's never given an interview to the Press, and I know she's a recluse, or very shy, or something . . .' I was gabbling like an idiot and all too aware of the fool I was making of myself, but for the first time in my life my charm and my looks, and even my nose for a story, weren't sufficient to cope with the situation. '. . . I came to do a story on Phoebe. The cartoonist. Is she in?'

The girl stared, and nodded, and smiled shyly, jumping down from the desk, walking round it on tiny ballet-dancer's feet, and finally sitting in the swivel chair, gesturing towards the piles of scattered papers in front of her.

'You came to talk about these?' she asked. There was a trace of a faint accent. Spanish? South American? She picked up a sheet of drawings in her tiny hand and waved them at me.

'Yes, please. I want to discuss the impact these cartoons are having at present, and their phenomenal success in America and Europe, and . . . Could I speak to Phoebe? Just for a moment? Really, I won't take much of her time,' I begged.

'But, I am Phoebe . . .' the girl said, quietly.

'You!' I gulped. 'But you're only a kid! Only a child. These cartoons, they're . . .'

I was going to say that they were the work of someone much older and wiser. They contained images of people, twisted and deformed, but each one a small spirit of hopeless rebellion, each one battling for space and understanding. They'd been called genius. They'd won awards, acclaim, syndication in thirty-odd countries.

'I'm seventeen,' she whispered. 'I draw what I see there, in the mirrors. I see you in the mirror. Two days, now.'

'Yes. I found out your address from a guy on a newspaper. I've been watching from over the road. I tried to get in to see you, but the caretaker downstairs said you never see anyone, and then he came across the road and told me I could come up,' I stammered.

'I sent for you. I liked you,' she smiled. The smile was sad and awkward, as if unused. 'You're very good-looking.'

'Do you mind if I sit down?' I asked.

My knees were rocky, my throat dry. I tried to piece the story together, a different story from the one I'd half-written in my head. 'All done by mirrors,' I rewrote, silently. Not the work of imagination at all, just a view of the world distorted by reflection, drawn by a child, a gauche prodigious child with the face of an angel, who now gestured towards a chair in the corner of the empty studio and continued to examine me with her mirror eyes.

But what was I worried about? I'd lost the original story, true, but I'd gained something else, something far more sensational. A kind of fraud, almost. This was more, far more, than an exercise in finding that difficult interview, more than just an assignment for a term's grades. It was a journalistic discovery, an exposure that would sell to the arty Sundays and the gutter Sundays. It would make my fortune. It would see me through into that job I was looking for on the nationals. It would make my name.

I ran my finger, moistly, inside the collar of my shirt, licked my lips, coughed and took a deep breath to steady my heartbeat. The girl stared like an unblinking china doll, waiting.

'So,' I asked. 'Can I write the story?'

She shrugged.

'What story?'

'Yours. How you started in the business. How you learned about the mirrors, you know . . .'

She made a small sound, between a laugh and a sigh.

'But there is no story. This is just what I do. I always did this. I've nothing to tell you. My name is Phoebe. I am an illustrator. I am seventeen. I work,' she said, baldly.

'Personal detail, that's what I need,' I told her. 'Like family, boyfriends, social interests, hobbies?'

She looked at me, blankly.

'Friends,' I said. 'You've got friends?' Friends are useful when you've got a dry subject. Friends dish the dirt and come up with the telling details that make the difference between story and sensation. But Phoebe shook her cloudy red hair and looked down at her slippers, then up at me again.

'I know no-one. Only the pictures,' she said, pointing to the mirrors. 'That's all. No parents, now. No friends. I'm from Argentina, so not very popular, no? This was the only way to survive. But it's gone now, hasn't it? You'll write a story about me, and people will say, "There, her cartoons are phoney. They're copied from mirror images. That's all." The immigration people will come round and find me. No-one will buy my work. It's over. I knew. As soon as I telephoned down to the caretaker and told him to let you in, I knew it was finished for me. You see, I'm not a mystery any more. I'm an illegal immigrant from an unpopular country, who fooled people. Look, look in the mirrors. It's like a fairground, huh? My father had a fairground. I used to play in the mirror room all the time, and draw what I saw. You could do it, too. In the mirrors everything is sad and funny at the same time, so it

78

looks like real life, because that's sad and funny at the same time. A child could do it. It's just a trick.'

And suddenly, the fairy was human. The girl sat surrounded by the busy contorted images, the street below, reflected over and over again into images of a pushy and overpopulated world fighting to crush the spark from us all. Crying.

I couldn't. I couldn't find it in my heart to go on taking notes. Like pulling the wings off a butterfly. She was lost and wretched, alien, and only trying to find a way, strange though her route was, through the crowds. I stood, walked across to her, and touched her small face with my fingertips. She said nothing, but leaned towards me, burying her head in my shoulder as I knelt at her side.

'It's OK, Phoebe,' I croaked. 'It's OK.' She was soft to hold, soft and vulnerable. And beautiful. Someone could love her. And someone could destroy her just as easily. But perhaps the most tragic thing was that she knew, despite her isolation, exactly what I represented, just that same human mix of sad and funny, love and destruction, that she saw in her mirrors and expressed in her cartoons.

'Come out with me tonight,' I asked, running my fingers through her tangle of hair. 'We'll have a meal, and there's this party on. I'll take you to that, eh? Meet a few people. You're a celebrity. Why not enjoy it?'

She shook her head and smiled.

'No, Nick. It's not worth it, is it? I think we both know that. Why don't you go now?'

'Please . . . ?' I argued.

'No. Go to your party. I've got some work to do, anyway,' she said.

She seemed perfectly composed. I think that's what finally decided me. Later I realized that it wasn't coldness, it was a kind of fatalistic acceptance, but at the time it felt to me like a light being switched off, almost as if her tears had worked the magic that was required and that now I was in the way. So, I collected my coat, and my notebook, and left.

I called in at the first pub I saw. It was too early in the evening and the place smelt of sour beer, stale smoke and acid bodies. Two old men sat hunched in one brown corner. A guy with cockatoo hair played the nudges on the fruit machine. A tired barmaid with lipsticked cheeks pulled me a tired pint, and I sat in the corner by the Gents and the telephone, trying to force it down. All the customers, through my confused eyes, turned into Phoebe's cartoon characters. She had made us all see the world on her terms. She was a strange girl. Lovely, too. It was tragic.

I rattled the loose change in my pocket and discovered two ten-pence pieces. Setting down the half-finished pint, I reached up to the nearest telephone and dialled a number from my notebook.

'Newsdesk,' a voice called, distantly.

'Listen,' I said. 'I've got this exclusive. Red-hot. My name's Nick Armstrong, and I'm a freelance. Can I come in and talk to you about this one? It's about the cartoonist, Phoebe. Yes. Front page, I reckon, but it'll cost you. I'm in the area. I could catch a cab and be with you in . . . oh . . . about five or ten minutes. OK? Nick Armstrong. Yes. I'll come straight round.'

The Other Half

Don't talk to me about how the other half live. I've met the other half. Her name is Natalie Ferguson, and I bumped into her last summer. God, how I envied that girl! She was my age, but she had everything most sixteen-year-old girls would give their eye-teeth for: looks, independence, a lifestyle that flowed in and out with the tide, and Bruce. But I'll come to Bruce, later. He was the one who put me right. I'd better start at the beginning, before I knew either of them existed.

My parents had rented a cottage on the South coast for August. I was furious. I wanted to go on a package to Tenerife or Corfu, even Majorca, but no, Mum has this fair skin which comes out in prickly heat in hot climates, and my kid sister Jo, who's eight and a pain, had inherited the same milky colouring. Dad works in London and it was his idea that, if we settled for Hastings for our holiday, we could take a month instead of two weeks. He'd join us at weekends for the first fortnight. It was all settled without so much as a 'What do you think, Beth?' which is typical of my parents' attitude. Like, I don't count. Or I didn't, then.

The thing that was really bugging me, apart from the obvious, was that I'd just set up quite a good opening with Jake Gamble, and I knew that if I was away for a month I'd slip out of his consciousness and someone else would slip in. The boys I know don't care a great deal for fidelity, or any of that 'only you' propaganda you hear so much about on pop records.

So there I was, stuck in a damp cottage, in the rain, near Hastings, with a demanding kid sister, no friends, no Jake, no freedom. Not much of a holiday. More a month of the worst days of your life. And we mustn't forget the GCSE results which were due out later in August and hung over me like a guillotine. You could say I was in a fairly negative mood, although Mum had rather stronger expressions for it than that, and the first few days consisted of a lot of shouting, stamping out of the cottage and door-banging, walking in the rain howling with self-pity, and tragic phone calls and postcards to Marie, Sarah and Kirsty, my friends at home.

Then I met Natti.

She was working in one of the arcades on the front, wearing a grubby sacking apron with compartments in it for change for the machines. Once seen, never forgotten. She had blonde hair piled up in a scrunchy heap on top of her head and frizzed to one side. She wore huge home-made hoop earrings and a strange dress with a nipped-in waist and a wide skirt crinolined with bright net underskirts. She chewed gum, had dirty hands and a grubby mark on her nose, but she looked astounding, the way I could have looked if I'd had the nerve or the face for it. But I'm tall and dark and, at the time, I was very sulky, too. Natti was sparkling with energy and backchat. Times I saw her fight back at a drunk or catch a passing put-down and throw it right back into someone's face.

Later that day I saw her again, at the Pizza Place.

She was in the Italian chalet-girl outfit all the other girls wore, but she moved faster, looked brighter, and that strange hairstyle and the perfect features separated her from the rest of the waitresses, despite the stupid uniform.

'I saw you earlier today,' I told her. 'At the arcade.'

'That's my day job. This is my night shift. For this week, anyway. Next week I might have a change. Might even have a rest. I've earned enough for the moment,' she grinned.

'Are jobs easy to find here?' I stammered, amazed by her casual attitude.

'If you know how,' she winked. 'I'm a resident, see. I live here. Got my own place. Got contacts.'

'Your own place?' I breathed.

'Caravan. Down by the shore,' she said, took my empty plate and raced to serve someone else.

I mulled over what she'd told me, and for the next two or three days I took my daily self-pitying walks along the shingle beach, looking at the rows of neatly parked mobile homes cluttering the shore-line. I wondered what that could be like, living alone in a caravan at my age, choosing to do what I wanted, not irritated by the teeny-bop synthetic music screaming from my sister's radio, not under-mined by my mother's irritation and sarcasm, just fending for myself, choosing to work or not to work without the necessary exam passes my dad kept on about. And on one of those solitary envious walks, I met Natti again.

It was the first day of sunshine we'd had. She was sitting cross-legged on a patch of deserted oily shingle, dressed in shorts and a baggy T-shirt, polishing shells.

'Hi,' I grunted, flopping down next to her. Sulky,

despite the bright sunlight. Mum and I had just had another episode of our daily row, and I'd thrown Jo's radio out of the window.

'Enjoying your holiday?' Natti laughed, as I groaned loudly.

I'd never walked as far as that along the shore. The neat sites with close-cropped grass and shiny cars, the sandy foreshores and little cafés had given way to something altogether scrubbier, more industrial. And behind us, on a ragged piece of debris-covered wasteland, was a single caravan.

It wasn't like the mobile homes I'd seen. It was a round, fat little caravan, dull, not metallic. It looked as if it was made from cardboard. The paintwork was scuffed, the door hung drunkenly, and one window was smashed.

'That where you live?' I asked. I mustn't have sounded very impressed.

'Home sweet home,' Natti smiled.

She looked as if she meant it, and later, after we'd talked for a while, I walked across the pebbles with her to examine it more closely. It really was a home sweet home, too, despite its funny outward appearance. Inside it was stuffed with cushions and soft toys and decorated with drawings and paintings. Brightly coloured curtains hung at the windows and matching covers were draped over the bench seating. Natti made us a coffee. I sank down into paradise.

That caravan had everything anyone could ever need. Natti said she had to collect water from a standpipe up by the road, and that she had to take showers at the public baths half a mile away, but there was a full-sized cooker, a calor-gas fridge, a portable stereo, racks of the most amazing records, and stacks of books and magazines. My mate Sarah had a fully fitted bedsit at home. Her dad's a builder and put a special extension on the house for her. But Natti's place would've knocked even Sarah's for six.

'This is incredible!' I kept saying.

I found myself spilling out to her all the grouses about the holiday, my parents, my sister, the exam results, Jake, and anything else I could think of. I'd been bottling most of it up for days, so being able to splurge it out while drinking someone else's coffee was a heady release.

'I'm having a holiday myself at the moment,' she said, 'so why don't you hang round for a day or two? I'll show you around, if you like.'

She was so confident, so self-assured, so full of instant laughter and easy conversation. She was wild, totally mad, knew everyone, knew everywhere to go. From that moment on, my holiday took off.

I was hardly ever in the cottage after that day. I spent every minute of every hour dragging round after Natti, discovering how to con food from the back doors of restaurants, how to talk myself into discos and private clubs. No doors were ever closed to her, and she let me through them, too. I was out until long after midnight, up early in the morning and ready for another crazy day. The longer I spent in Natti's company, the more I realized that the life I'd been leading tied me up in knots and was destroying my identity. My family was too demanding. My mother kept on and on at me about where I was going, and what I was doing, and why I couldn't spend more time with Jo. My father insisted I ate Sunday lunch with them and went on this boat trip he'd organized. One day I was forced out on a sightseeing tour which really was the most boring day I'd spent in my entire life, stuck on a coach with a load of pensioners, having to trek round dismal stately homes.

'You're showing me up,' my mother kept hissing at me. 'Why're you chewing gum? And why've you got those things in your hair? And will you stop annoying your sister!' The usual stuff, really.

It was such a change to get back to Natti's caravan. I told her about the trip and had her in fits, then we went out on the town again.

There was only one thing I couldn't quite understand. Natti and boys. Sometimes, usually in fact, we'd pick up a couple of holidaymakers, but there was nothing much more than a laugh and some suggestive come-ons that never got us anywhere. There was a moment, some time as the night drew on, when Natti's quick-fire backchat would stop and when she'd pull away from a touch or a kiss with something like a shudder.

'What's up?' I asked one night when, on Natti's whispered instructions to me, we'd left two boys standing in the disco while we disappeared by way of an emergency exit. 'Yours was fantastic, and mine was better than usual.'

'There's this boy. He hangs around, sometimes . . .' she stammered, for the first time at a loss for a throw-away comment.

Bruce. One day, when I arrived at the caravan, he was there.

I didn't quite understand Natti's devotion at first. Bruce wasn't remarkable to look at. His nose was too long, his eyes too dark, his mouth slightly misshapen. He was skinny and tall, with legs that looked as if they could fold up into several concertina creases, and he had an odd way of dressing: jacket too small, trousers too large. That was first impressions. But as he spoke, as I listened, his voice had a hypnotic quietening quality, and his eyes a depth of understanding and gentleness I'd never experienced before. I began to think of him as the best-looking boy I'd ever met. I don't know why. It was worrying. I was trying to tell Natti about the row I'd had with Jo and my dad, but Bruce kept looking at me. Staring. I had this odd sensation that he didn't like me very much, and I wanted to impress him. I kept talking and talking.

'Let's go to the fair,' he said suddenly, taking my hand. His hand was cool. My hand tingled. I remember that I wanted him then. I remember almost a silent scream as I looked at him and looked at Natti and hated her for having everything I wanted and nothing I could take or borrow. Except him.

The feeling wouldn't go away. He held my hand, and Natti's, as we walked either side of him. It seemed so unfair. He was obviously close to Natti, yet she treated him with a kind of smiling in-difference; not the same as the strange, almost neurotic rejection she dealt out to other boys, but almost as if she took him, distantly, for granted. I wouldn't. I could love him.

I spent the whole afternoon in a turmoil of rides and emotions. I watched Natti, waiting for a sign from her that Bruce was a needed possession, but she was as casual as ever. There was warmth when she looked at him. That was all. I edged close to him on the waltzers, held his hand on the big dipper while she waited at the bottom for us, and when we emerged, glowing from the screaming, Bruce went down to where she was standing, pale and anxious.

'Kiss me,' he smiled, offering his lips.

Natti turned gently away.

'I'll kiss you!' I laughed, taking hold of his hollow-cheeked face in both my hands and pulling it roughly towards mine.

'No!' Natti screamed. 'No! Don't!' And then she ran, a blur of rainbow colours into the crowds, sobbing hysterically.

'What . . . ?' I stammered.

Bruce pushed me away furiously.

'What did you do that for? Why did you hurt her like that? How could you do it?' he yelled at me.

I must have looked as dumbstruck as I felt.

'You do know, don't you?' he asked. 'You do know about Natti? You know I'm all she's got!'

'Don't be ridiculous. Natti's got everything,' I blustered, embarrassed by this terrifying anger and rejection.

'So she didn't tell you? Or maybe you didn't listen. No, you're not the type to listen, are you? Nice cosy existence, nice comfy things to moan about, like little rows with your loving family and little problems with getting the most out of your holiday! So you thought you'd add a little holiday romance to your shopping list, did you? You want everything!' he hissed.

'Natti's *got* everything,' I repeated weakly.

'Everything? A dad who attacked her repeatedly, a mum who threw her out, a loneliness you've never known? Natti *has* to live the way she lives. She just makes the best of everything. And I'm trying to get her to trust men again, but . . .' he shook his head despairingly and raced off into the crowds to look for Natti.

I stood there with the stupid fairground music blaring round me, the candyfloss and toffee apples, rifle fire and screams and laughter, staring after them both.

Like I said, I know about how the other half live: Natalie Ferguson, making the best of nothing much to live for, and I'd envied her.

Perhaps, in a way, I still do.

Hens

By the time we arrived at Boogy's on that Friday night, the place was full to bursting, and so were we. We'd already been for an Indian meal, and we'd had chicken biryani that had sultanas in it, so I'd had to leave those on the side of my plate, and chips, and some funny chutneys, and Mrs Whittaker, who told me that I had to call her Madge, ordered some poppadoms and some stuffed nan, but I didn't eat any of that because it looked even funnier than it sounded. Janine couldn't stop laughing about that name. Kath bought three bottles of wine to share between the six of us and then packed us into two taxis to go just down the road to the club, and I was already feeling a bit light-headed.

Friday isn't usually hen night at Boogy's. I'd been there once before on a Friday, and it was the same as any other Friday-night place, where you sit around and look hopeful and go home in tears because your best friend's got off with someone and you've not. At least, that's what usually happens to me. I'd really like to be Passionate Paula, but I'm actually Paula, Poor Kid. I think that's why Kath invited me to her wedding, and to the hen night, to make me feel like part of it all. I'd only been working at the shop since summer, and Kath had been dead nice. So had Mrs Whittaker, and Janine, the one with the limp and the jokes. They were both invited. And there was Michelle, Kath's older sister, and Jo, who was Keith's sister. Keith was the one Kath was getting married to on the Saturday morning. I'd only seen him a couple of times, but he had the sort of looks that send your legs out of action. Unbelievable. He was my ideal, was Keith, but, as Nick pointed out when he finished with me in May, I'm not the sort of girl that ideal boys would be seen dead with, so I don't suppose he noticed me. Keith, that is. Mind you, Nick only noticed me for a fortnight between getting ditched by Anne Francis and going out with her again. But I'm going off the point, aren't I? That's my problem. I dream and drift off. And I go on and on without stopping for breath. Kath says I haven't caught up with real life yet, and maybe she's right.

There we were, anyway, piling into Boogy's, all a bit giggly and having to pay the full admission because it was after nine-thirty and not really hen night, but the DJ must have been warned, because as soon as we came out of the cloakroom and started walking towards our reserved table, right at the front, he faded the record on the turntable and put on this tape of the 'Wedding March'. We hadn't even got settled in our seats before he dragged Kath up on to the stage and made her drink a vodka and tonic in one swallow. Then he asked her where she was going for her honeymoon, and when she said Benidorm he made her sing this duet of 'Viva España' with him. It was so funny that I was nearly wetting myself. Kath hasn't got much of a singing voice, and he kept tickling her with this rose he was holding between his teeth, so you can imagine.

Then he put this garter on her. That was a bit risky, but everyone was laughing and whooping, even Kath. If it'd been me, though, I'd've crawled inside one of the amps in embarrassment, I would. I don't like being shown up. When I whispered that to Mrs Whittaker . . . Madge . . . she said it was just my age, and that I'd grow out of it. That's what everyone keeps saying to me, as if being sixteen's a disease or a school uniform or a bunk bed. Kath came down off the stage then with a wrapped present that turned out to be a pair of pink frilly knickers, and bought us all a drink while we passed the knickers round and Janine made jokes.

'I think getting married's really romantic, don't you, Madge?' I said.

Janine nudged me in the back and hissed, 'She's divorced,' down my ear. Shown up again. I nearly died. But Mrs Whittaker just smiled and said, 'While it lasts,' and then Michelle dragged us all up to do that stupid dance with all the mad actions. It was a big laugh. Janine wasn't too steady on her legs, and Jo kept singing all the wrong words, and Mrs Whittaker didn't know it at all and just did hokey-cokey actions, but when we came to the bit about pretending your name is Keith, which is one of the stupid lines in the stupid song, Kath suddenly went all floppy, right on to Michelle, and burst into tears.

I didn't know what to do. I was right in the middle of the bit before that, because I'd got left behind, even though I was only drinking lemon and lime. I stopped dead.

'What's up?' I asked Jo.

'They had a row last night,' she grunted. 'Her and him. He went out with the lads instead of turning up at St Mary's for the rehearsal. She went spare. And no wonder. They're all pigs. My Paul went off, too, and he's supposed to be best man!'

'Pigs,' Mrs Whittaker echoed, thickly.

'Thought his stag night was tonight?' Janine murmured.

'Is . . . ? Oh heck!' Jo gulped.

We all looked in the direction she was looking. And there he was. Keith. And his stag night. And this kissogram girl. I suppose she was a kissogram girl, anyway, because she didn't have enough on to be just someone he'd brought in from the pub. She had her arms round his neck, and he looked as if he thought she was just a meat pie on legs, because he was making a right meal of her.

'No!' Janine squealed, standing in front of them all and spreading her spindly arms out to hide them from Kath, who was having drinks poured down her by Michelle.

'Paul Wilson! Haven't you got enough sense to keep away from here after last night?' Jo started screaming, picking up all the handbags we'd put in the middle of our dance, and throwing them, one by one, at his head. Madge salvaged hers, but mine bounced off his ear and on to the floor where it split open, and all my things went flying. There were personal things in there, you know, and I didn't know where to put myself. I just flew down, spreadeagled myself over the lot so nobody would see the Snoopy I'd had since I was about thirteen, and the photograph of Mick that I'd drawn a Hitler moustache on, and all the other things. I was trying to wriggle my hands under my body to collect everything together when these shoes appeared by my nose, and this lad, from the stag party, bent down and handed me my keyring and said, 'It's Paula Samuels, isn't it?'

I didn't recognize him at first. It was hardly any wonder with the screaming that was going on over our heads, and the fact that my glasses were

94

somewhere under my knee and felt a bit smashed. Madge had persuaded me to take them off earlier, in the Koh-i-Noor, and put them in my bag because she said I looked a lot better without them. I'd only agreed because it blurred the sultanas a bit and I'm not too bad with sultanas if I can't actually see them. I regretted taking them off now, I can tell you.

'Pete Russell. I was in the same General Science group at the high school. I work with Keith,' he prompted.

'Oh yeah,' I remembered. I'd been fairly crazy about him, months back. He had freckles, and a gap between his front teeth that was very sexy when he smiled. But I felt a fool lying there, trying to pretend we were having a normal 'Do you remember?' sort of conversation while the destruction of the world as we know it was going on over my head. I managed to shove everything in my bag and was on my knees, being dragged to my feet by Pete Russell, when Kath suddenly saw what all the aggro was about.

She stood up and howled like an American werewolf. I hid behind Pete as she came diving over and hurled herself at the meat pie in suspenders.

'Kath . . .' Mrs Whittaker appealed.

'Clobber 'er!' Michelle yelled.

'. . . And here's Dire Straits . . .' the DJ muttered down his mike.

'I'll help!' Janine squealed, going for Keith's ankles.

I needed to go to the bathroom. I get very anxious, sometimes. I'm a very non-violent person, and I have thought of becoming a vegetarian because I go all woozy if I see blood, even if it's coming out of dead meat, and I could sense there was going to be bloodshed. I dashed off through the door marked 'Ladies' and hung over a washbasin for a while, trying to bring myself round. I splashed my face, and rinsed my mouth out, but I looked very strange in my reflection, what with being so pale, and having no glasses on, and my hair all fuzzed out with excitement.

Pete Russell was waiting for me outside the cloakroom door.

'I was worried about you,' he said.

I thought that was a really nice thing to say. Kath was bashing the kissogram girl over the head with one of her shoes, and bashing Keith over the head with the other.

'Going to the wedding?' Pete asked.

'What wedding?' I asked dully.

'Because, maybe I could take you for a drink afterwards?' he said, ignoring my depressive question.

I looked up at his freckles and gappy teeth. I really liked him. But, in the circumstances . . .

'It wouldn't work,' I said.

'What wouldn't?'

'Love,' I said. Maybe I hadn't been drinking just lemon and lime after all.

'Oh, take no notice of that lot,' he laughed, gesturing towards where the bouncers were trying to break it up between the bride and groom. 'It's ups and downs. That's just a down. The downs don't last long.'

'Oh no?' Madge Whittaker asked, sliding past him into the cloakroom. 'It's all downhill, Sunshine!'

'See you tomorrow!' Pete whispered, squeezing my hand before running after the heap in the doorway made up of Keith and Paul and a kissogram girl.

*

96

It was a lovely wedding. Lovely. The sky was clear blue, the sun shone, and Kath looked so beautiful I had to cry over and over again. They did make a nice couple. Perfect. Just like the little bride and groom on the cake they cut together before driving off, cuddling, to Benidorm.

Pete Russell lent me his hankie and bought me two lemon and limes that made me feel glowing inside.

'Well?' he asked.

'Well what?'

'See you tomorrow?'

'Could do,' I said.

Inside

Annemarie was uneasy. There was nothing, quite, which she could put her finger on. Outwardly the signs were that she was very much the self she had always been: perfectly attractive, popular and contented. She wore her long blonde hair tied back into a plait for college, relieving the severity with huge bright earrings, and wore it loose and tangled in the evenings for partying and socializing. But, just at the moment, it felt tight; felt as if it pulled at her scalp and forehead in its neat single plait. In the evenings it felt heavy and untidy. Yet people continued to admire its gold brilliance, as if they saw nothing wrong. But then, they wouldn't. She had worked hard to create the seamless mask she hid behind. No-one really knew what was going on inside another person, or indeed what the inside might be like, given the opportunity to examine it. Annemarie's inside was tired, bored and uncertain under the even smiles. She needed . . .

Excitement. That was it. The last two relationships in her life had been damp squibs. There had been no spirit of adventure in either of the boys, no passion, no sadness when it was all over. She needed something to give edge and meaning to her life, as love, real love, often does. She needed to tremble and giggle, be carried away, forget about the dullness of routine in someone's arms, or some-one's need. None of that had happened for months. As she listened to the other girls exchanging week-end experiences in the Monday-morning break, she resented not being able to contribute or enthuse. There was no-one in her life, nothing to form a focal point of her day, or her week. The others were discussing the possibilities for next week's Easter disco.

'Are you coming, Annemarie?' Karen asked.

She shrugged, 'Who with?'

'With your looks, you don't have to drag some-one along!' Lucy sighed. 'You'll pick someone up.' There was good reason for her to sigh. Annemarie had picked up, and dropped, Lucy's boyfriend only a couple of months ago.

'Not really what I want at the moment,' Anne-marie explained, groping for the words, trying to explain. 'I want something special to happen, not just the usual meat-market parade. I'm looking for something different this time.'

'The love of your life?' Karen giggled.

'Maybe. Maybe not. Just something out of the ordinary,' she stammered.

'Quasimodo? The Phantom of the Opera? Jack the Ripper?' Lucy sneered.

'No . . . but . . .' Annemarie considered, twirling one of her brass hoop earrings, thinking. Lucy had just given her the germ of an idea. Who needed love? Fun, change, a good laugh would brighten things up.

'I know,' she breathed. 'I'll ask Ken to take me.'

'Ken!' Karen squealed, then put her hand over her mouth in embarrassment as everyone in the coffee bar turned to look at where the squeal came from, and Annemarie put her finger to her lips.

'Ken?' Karen repeated in a whisper. 'Not Ken the oink? You couldn't! Why would you want to?'

'Why not?' Annemarie asked quietly, her mouth curling round a private smile. 'At least he'd be grateful for a chance to go out with me. He wouldn't take me for granted, not him. It'd be really funny, too, wouldn't it? To walk in there with him? I can just see their faces!'

'No, Annemarie. It's not fair,' Lucy complained, smiling a little, despite herself, at the thought of the princess and the frog.

'It is fair! Why not? You don't have to be madly in love with someone to ask them out, do you? You can ask someone out for all sorts of different reasons. And I'm asking him out to . . .'

'Make fun of him,' Lucy interrupted.

'Not exactly. Maybe to give him a night to remember, huh?' Annemarie answered.

The idea, so casually suggested, began to appeal to her. Ken was the college idiot, a gawky lanky boy with large ears and that rosy-coloured skin left by acne treatment and too-frequent blushing. He rarely spoke. Hidden in the corner of Art and Graphics classes, creating goodness-knows-what behind the barrier of his drawing-board, he'd long been a butt of the girls' jokes. No other boy took Art and Graphics. No other boy scuttled away, as he did, whenever the girls approached, or hid behind thick paperbacks in the coffee bar. He wore jumbo cords and Morrissey shirts and obviously cut his own copper-coloured hair. He wasn't exactly weird, merely apart from the mainstream of college life.

'I'll ask him, today,' Annemarie announced. 'In our Graphics class.'

'He'll think it's his birthday!' Karen giggled.

'He'll blush,' Lucy said.

'He won't know what's hit him,' Annemarie grinned. 'So what do I wear for a date with Ken? A guernsey sweater and a floral skirt?'

'A sou'wester and a dustbin bag?' Karen suggested.

'White. I'll wear white. That'll provide a nice contrast to all his redness. We'll look suitably different from each other. It's a good joke,' Annemarie laughed.

Already she could imagine the evening. They would walk in together, she in her plain white short dress, with her pale gold hair sleek and loose, he in his creased navy cords, black off-the-shoulder shirt and brilliant flame face and hair, stooping and awkward. It would make her feel good not to be on the arm of some regular-featured, perfect man whose eyes and hands might roam during the evening. Ken would keep his eyes fixed on her. Ken would be grateful, impressed and submissive. It would be an adventure.

Ken was already installed in the Art room when the girls walked in, Karen giggling behind Annemarie, Lucy trailing in the rear, a little embarrassed by the whole thing. Annemarie, she believed, would tire of this idea before Friday and leave Ken dangling from her heartstrings. She would never go through with it, never actually walk into a college disco with someone who had, for so long, been a laughing stock. She could have anyone. Probably, before Friday, she would find her anyone, just as she'd found Graham. Lucy still ached when she remembered Graham. He'd been the best-looking boy who had ever taken an interest in her – for four days, until, while waiting for Lucy to come out of an evening class, he'd bumped into Annemarie who had offered to keep him company. And that had been the end. Annemarie could eat men alive. Lucy didn't relish the prospect of watching this particular demonstration of that ability.

She and Karen slid into their seats, watching Annemarie curve her way through the chaos of drawing-boards and easels towards the bent copper-coloured head and the silence of concentration which surrounded the college idiot.

'Ken,' Annemarie announced, rather than said. Her voice carried. It was a clear high voice with just a slight grating edge of huskiness.

'Uh?'

The boy looked up from his drawing-board, startled. He hadn't seen or heard her approach. He blushed, as predicted, his rosy face glowing more brightly than ever.

'Ken, there's a disco, as you know, at the college on Friday night,' Annemarie said brightly, 'and I'd be more than grateful if you'd do me the honour of coming to that disco with me.'

'She's laying it on a bit thick,' Karen giggled, quietly, in Lucy's ear.

'Oh, you would, would you?' Ken asked.

The girls had never heard him speak before. His voice was different from what they'd imagined. It was melodic, vibrant, not the nervy muttering they had believed would be dragged from him. And his face was different, too, as he looked up at Anne-marie's intrusion. Despite the blush, there was a slight upturn of one corner of his full mouth, a glinting mockery, a hint of amusement in his brown eyes.

'Y . . . Yes,' Annemarie stammered, looking distinctly apprehensive.

'Terribly sorry to disappoint you,' Ken smiled,

103

'but no. You're not my type. You've got no fire, no purpose, have you? You have to feed off other people. You're not feeding off me, Annemarie.'

There was a trembling silence. Annemarie stared. Her eyes filled, unexpectedly, with tears. Karen coughed, picking up a pencil, bowed her head over the drawing-board in embarrassment. Lucy stared at the two of them, no longer predator and victim, or at least not in the expected order. Ken's smile was gentle.

'Sorry,' he murmured.

Annemarie turned on her heel and ran from the Graphics class. Her hair pulled at her face. She loosened the elastic band which tied it back, combed at the plait wildly with her fingers as she tore down the corridor and hurled herself into the cloakroom, burning with the insult. To have been rejected by him, by Ken of all people, for him to have dared to assess her, to have the presumption to pierce the mask and lay bare the emptiness inside . . . !

But, in the Art room, Lucy's stare did not falter. She held her eyes steady, focused on something she had never noticed before. And Ken stared unashamedly back at her, smiling his gentle smile . . .

Seeing, Believing

Josie was annoyed to discover, on that clear blue morning in June, that two people had taken up position on her beach.

She thought of it as her beach, although its existence was known to other locals. It was a clear white horseshoe of sand surrounded by dark rocks which divided and separated the tiny bay into several private areas. To reach it, a long walk along the cliff-tops was necessary, through gorse and heather which ripped at bare legs and overgrew the paths that must have existed once upon a time. Even most of the locals preferred to take their sun on the more easily accessible bays closer to the town. Josie, though, was willing to trek the two miles or so through the undergrowth to reach Soapy Cove.

That morning, the white sand was disfigured by two brown bodies.

Josie stood silently on the cliff edge, looking down at them and beyond to where the sea stretched out to the misty edge of the sky. She frowned. She needed privacy. She wanted to make notes in her notebook. Josie had decided that her future was as a writer when she left school. She had read that writers were lonely observers, people who watched life instead of joining in with it. This described her exactly. Throughout the long summer holidays she'd been alone, friendless. Now there were two intruders into her solitude.

There was the barely distinguishable path to the beach, down the cliff, at her feet. To have taken it would have meant parading in full view of the two close bodies. What if they spoke to her? The question didn't bear thinking about.

To the right, two hundred yards or so away, was another, less obvious route. It did not lead down to the main expanse of clear clean sand, but to an offshoot of it, a small patch protected by a fence of sleek black rock. The smaller beach was less attractive. The sea, just there, was spiked with rocks and dangerous for swimming. But it would have to do.

Josie made her way carefully through the bracken to the second pathway. She watched the couple. They didn't look up, or move. She hadn't been observed. Some people, though, had no real gift for seeing. She did. Appearances, movement, surfaces, reaction, all these mattered to her. What people were seen to *do,* she had learned was often more important than what they *said.* That's what she would write about.

She slid down the path, taking great care to place herself so that her movements disturbed nothing. Soon, she established herself behind the rock wall, her towel spread on the sand, her notebook and sandwiches unpacked from her haversack, her shorts and top removed to reveal the brief purple bikini. Purple was her favourite colour. It had mood and vibration. It sang. She liked to dress in purple, although some people, her mother included, tried to tell her that too much of a good thing was too harsh on the eyes. What they were trying to tell her, Josie knew, because you could only trust their eyes, not their words, was that she wasn't attractive enough to carry it off.

She lay full length on her towel, positioning herself so that she was hidden from the couple on the main beach but had a view of them through a gap in the rocks. They were framed, as if through a camera viewfinder, by the sharp angles of rocks.

But they presented no sharp angles. Lithe and tanned, only a few steps away from her, they cuddled, giggled and whispered, chased each other into the sea, dived from rocks, and collapsed exhausted into each other's arms.

The girl was beautiful. She had shoulder-length, red crimped hair – no, not red but a kind of bruised-plum shade with rosy highlights. Her face was perfect, wide-eyed, full-lipped, smoothly contoured. But it was the boy who took Josie's full attention. Dressed only in a pair of tennis shorts, he had that sculptured look of a bronze statue. Every feature was classically perfect and innocent. His soft dark hair was rather longer than the present fashion, but something about the cut suggested good taste and good breeding. That much was obvious.

Josie dreamed. Her mother always said that she had a powerful imagination. But she'd needed something to trigger it off. He did. She decided that his name was Miles. He was a romantic hero, perhaps a young doctor – no, a young art-dealer – fabulously wealthy, orphaned, heir to a great estate. That was what she would write.

The girl who curled in his arms and threw back her long plum-coloured hair as he whispered in her ear would be called Victoria. She looked like a Victoria. She was tall, slim and scented. Her perfume, carried on a warm breeze, drifted across to Josie as the girl unpacked a small picnic. Her summer dress lay at her feet like a golden puddle. She wore a yellow bikini. She had to be a secretary, or a waitress. Despite the beauty, there was something Josie's mother would call 'a little vulgar' in the frilly bikini, and in the heavy perfume.

Josie watched, hating the girl. She would make Victoria into a gold-digger, a girl with a murky past and a passion for the young art-dealer's money. She would create, for Victoria, an extravagant plot to seduce the rich orphan and milk him of his inheritance. Why couldn't a boy like that fall in love with her? Why were perfect men like Miles so easily fooled by scheming women? She'd read a book with that kind of plot at the beginning of the holidays, but it helped to see the kind of character you'd read about.

Josie wrote quickly, jotting down the main characters in her first blockbusting novel. This would make her fortune. There was Miles, the hero, the innocent. There was Victoria, the temptress. And there was Victoria's real boyfriend, an Italian pop-star who needed to fund his fading career. Then there was the beautiful Justine, Miles' childhood sweetheart, convent-educated, pure as the driven snow, a girl with a secret illness which made her hide away from the world, but who would come to the rescue of her true love when the time was right. What a story!

Josie put her pen down and dozed, warmed and lulled by the sun. The couple packed away the picnic, dressed, talked . . .

'Tomorrow, Martin?' the girl asked.

'Tomorrow could be difficult. You know my situation. I'm not making excuses for myself, Vinnie, but you know how it is. Let's say Wednesday. And look, I bought you this . . .'

He pulled out from a carrier bag by his side, a purple shawl, garishly printed with large yellow marigolds, and draped it round her shoulders.

'. . . I thought it was your sort of thing,' he explained, tipping her face up to his, kissing her quickly.

Vinnie shivered and pulled the shawl closer.

'I wish it wasn't like this,' she sighed.

'So do I. Believe me, so do I!' he murmured.

Josie didn't hear this exchange. She couldn't have done. She slept, her head on her notebook, her observant eyes closed against the light of the sun. But she had the seeds of her big novel. The intruders on the beach had provided it.

The next day, she waited in vain for their return. She needed inspiration. She had dreamed, embroidered and filled out the plot. The problem was in knowing how to start writing. She needed to see again and smell again to give herself the clues into the words that would bring the intrigue to life. But she was alone on the beach all day, resigned to her small quiet corner behind the rock wall. She invented reasons. Perhaps there could be a tragic car crash. Perhaps the temptress could have a scene, just here, with the sultry Italian pop-star. 'Victoria' could have been delayed by her real lover, while the wealthy orphan lay mangled in the wreck of his Porsche.

No! The thought terrified her. Miles must remain whole and untouched, as perfect a hero as ever slid across the pages of the interminable paperback romances she read. He must be the best. He *was* the best. She lay stretched in the sun, remembering the definition of his tanned muscles, remembering the sweet gentleness of his lazy brown eyes, in love for the first time with someone she had seen and almost reached out to touch. He was the hero of her book. But he was the love of her life. He filled all her sun-baked dreaming and whispered 'Justine' into her ear. Justine. The name suited her. It was elegant, without being flashy. If they ever made a mini-series of her novel, she'd insist that she played the part of Justine.

On Wednesday the couple was there again, and on Sunday afternoon, and on Monday. By the second week she had grown accustomed to their pattern, and would reach the beach before they did and hide in her small corner, notebook poised, adding detail to the already complex plot.

She discovered, parked in the coast road at the nearest access to the beach, a dusty motorbike and, some distance away, a small racing cycle. His and hers. Josie found them one Wednesday when she'd had to scramble from the beach before she gave herself away. She had almost called out, 'She doesn't love you, Miles. But I do!' It was strange how real this story had become for her. It was taking over her whole life. But she had realized, just in time, what she was about to do and had scrambled away during their picnic, packing her sandwiches and notebook into her rucksack so hastily, scrambling up the dangerously steep path so noisily, that Vinnie had held her breath.

'Listen!' she'd said. And then, 'Oh, listen. Stop a minute and listen.'

'What? Look, we haven't much time. I have to be back in town by five,' he'd argued, too reluctant to waste the moment to turn to see a slim girl with a rucksack scrambling up the cliffs. So he didn't see Josie.

'Time! That's all you think about, these days!' Vinnie cried. 'Time to meet her from work, time for me to disappear. Time to hide. Time to get me out of your life.'

'It's not like that, love,' he whispered, aware that the situation was turning, like the tide, against him. 'I love you. I care. I bought you a hat.'

'Great!' she sobbed, pulling the wide-brimmed straw hat over her plum curls. 'I get a hat. She gets you!'

'Maybe things could be different,' Martin sighed.

'They won't be,' Vinnie said, decisively. She had known other girls in her situation. It never worked out. And yet, sometimes, she knew that he cared and that he would miss her when she made the painful decision to leave him. He would miss her as he would miss sunshine and quiet, this quiet spot, this secret two-timing romance.

Josie returned home and examined herself in the bedroom mirror. Love had added a shine to her eyes, making her almost attractive. But not really. She couldn't quite persuade herself that Justine looked as boring as this. If she was to identify with the character of Justine, she had to work on her a little. Josie stared at her flat, long dark hair. Men didn't like flat, long dark hair. Men like Miles fell for curls and reddish rinses. She considered carefully before setting out to the chemist.

On Sunday the beach was almost deserted. Almost, but not quite. Josie looked down from the top of the cliff, expecting to see empty sand, sky and sea and saw instead a pile of something bright, topped by a floppy straw hat and a white piece of paper held down by a flat black stone. She looked round

111

anxiously, expecting to see the couple arrive at any moment. Yet it was too early for their meeting. She could take the safe path and investigate. Pushing her newly crimped, plum-coloured hair behind her ears, she raced down towards the waves' edge and rescued the pile before the abnormally high tide rolled it away. There was a purple scarf, printed with yellow marigolds, a large floppy straw hat, and a note . . .

'M,' it said. 'Please take back the things you gave me. I've been offered a job in Scotland. It's the best way. You never had a heart, did you? How could you do it? V.'

Josie stared at the note which made nonsense of her novel plot. She tried to accommodate the new details. Victoria, after all, couldn't be the temptress. Not if she wrote desperate notes like this one. She had to be a real heroine, one with a heart-breaking role to play. Novels were more complicated to write than Josie had thought. Taking the scarf and the hat in her arms, she withdrew to her hideaway behind the rocks, and tried to rewrite. But Victoria as heroine didn't fit in with the plots of the love stories she'd read. The girl wasn't a hard woman of the world, as you were supposed to be if you had secret seductive meetings with heroic men on deserted beaches. She was just a kid in love, hopelessly. A kid like Josie herself. Someone who felt she had to run away and hide because no-one loved her enough.

She sat reworking the plot frantically until sunset. Miles didn't arrive. Perhaps Victoria hadn't really expected him to. Perhaps she had known that, for him, the affair was played out. She'd been the noble one. He, the one Josie had thought was innocent, was really a rat. And Josie, who had throughout her life believed that things are exactly as they appear, if you look hard enough, now had the dawning realization of the deception that appearance offers. People pretended, played a part.

And as realization came, so did the words. She threw away the complicated plot and began to write about reality, feelings, complications. For days she didn't leave the house. She sat curled up in her room, filling sheet after sheet of paper with something that, although awkward and a little childish, poorly expressed and stumbling in places, was the tentative beginnings of a first novel.

When, finally, she ventured out, her plum curls flying, the floppy straw hat on her head, the scarf thrown casually across one shoulder, it was to celebrate the completion of the first chapter, written and rewritten, of her novel, *Victoria*. Josie had now identified totally with Victoria. Through the summer evening crowds she marched proudly, ignoring the stares of drunken holidaymakers who were stunned into silence by her eccentric but undeniable good looks. She ignored the calls, the shouts, the offers. She didn't see or hear the sculptured boy who stood as still as a rock in the moving tide of people, screaming after her as she passed by.

'Vinnie! Vinnie!' He watched her plum-coloured curls bouncing under the straw hat, the shawl he had bought billowing out behind her.

'Who's Vinnie?' the sharp-eyed little blonde asked, grabbing his arm before he could run after her. Her grip was like a vice. 'Is she that girl you were seeing behind my back, weeks ago?'

'You . . . you knew?' he stammered, his mouth trembling, weakly.

'Of course I knew. Went to see her. Got rid of her, didn't I?' the girl sneered.

She laughed wickedly, still hanging on to Martin's arm. He couldn't move. He stared after the disappearing girl, his eyes brimming with tears, torn apart between duty to this vicious little blonde and the girl he had always loved with an overwhelming passion. Vinnie.

'Told her how you crippled me in that motorbike accident, and how you owed me something, didn't I?' the blonde sneered.

Then she turned him round so that he couldn't see what he missed so bitterly, and pulled him along by her side, exaggerating her limp to exaggerate his guilt.

Josie moved on through the crowds, working on Chapter Two, the chapter where the beautiful Victoria meets this innocent-looking but wicked seductive rat, Miles. Josie would make the Miles character so attractively evil that the whole world would love and forgive Victoria her moment of passion.

Funny, she thought, how things are never quite as they appear. Now, she could see through everything. She was a real writer.

✳ Hide and Seek

Halfway up High Street, Rachel suddenly announced, 'Wait for me here, eh? I'm just nipping into the Ladies!'

'The film starts in five minutes!' Michelle argued. 'And, anyway, there's a loo in the cinema!'

'Must dash. Wait here,' was all Rachel shouted, over her shoulder, as if she hadn't heard.

Emma looked from Rachel to Michelle, waiting for the explosion. Michelle was a demolition expert, given the opportunity to raise her voice a little. Emma scrunched up inside, waiting for the howls of rage.

But Michelle didn't rage. She smiled and grabbed Emma's arm.

'Quick, let's go!' she hissed.

'What?'

'Let's get out of here while we've got the chance. Come on. You didn't want to see the film anyway, did you? Good! Now let's get rid of Rachel Wilson. I know this bistro place we can go to and . . .' Michelle blurted, pulling Emma along after her.

'Just a minute,' Emma stammered, shaking Michelle's pudgy hand from her arm. 'Yes, I do want to see the film and, anyway, it's not right, leaving Rachel.'

' "It's not right leaving Rachel," ' Michelle

mimicked in a prissy little voice. 'Listen, that girl's done worse things to me in her time, and this is an emergency!'

'I'm staying,' Emma said, firmly, standing her ground for once.

Michelle was obviously surprised. She was used to Emma trailing along, no matter what, like a little pet gerbil. But the rebellion suited Michelle very well. Very well indeed.

'Right then. Please yourself! I'm off,' she smirked, powering across High Street on her plump little legs and her fragile little high-heeled shoes.

Rachel slipped into the High Street Ladies and out again through the Church Street exit. She had planned this to perfection. She giggled to herself, thinking of that fat Michelle, and the pathetic little Emma, standing like two lost bus-stops on High Street, waiting for her.

She'd had no intention of going to the pictures. None at all. Honestly! Michelle was so stupid that she couldn't even see Rachel was all made-up with fake tan stuff and squeezed into a white cotton knee-skimming dress that had cost her an arm and a leg. Would she dress up like that for the pictures? No way. She'd'd've dressed up like Emma, in jeans and a T-shirt. But she'd've looked a million times better than Emma, even if she did say so herself.

She grinned along Church Street, patting her hair, and checked her reflection in the shop windows as she passed. Knock out. The blonde highlights did wonders for her. Tonight was the night.

'Eat your heart out, Craig Eddlestone,' she gurgled to herself. 'I'm coming to get you!'

*

Michelle plodded round the back of the parish church, regretting the shoes. They were white, sort of pointed, with tiny shapely heels. The shop assistant this morning had told her that they added contours to her ankles and slimmed her legs down beautifully. What she hadn't added was that they'd squeeze her toes up like wheel clamps and that within five minutes of trying to walk in them she'd wish she'd never been born.

Michelle winced as she tried to negotiate the cobblestones. But she knew that you have to suffer to be beautiful. And, although she hadn't in her wildest dreams imagined she'd be given a chance in a million, this very night, to make her dreams come true, she'd dressed up, just in case she happened to bump into him on the way to the pictures. Now, though . . . now, the whole pattern of the evening had changed. She'd grabbed the opportunity with both feet. She knew exactly where to head for. Didn't he usually pop in there around eight? Wasn't that what the waiter with the horse teeth had told them last night?

'Isn't that Craig Eddlestone?' Rachel had asked Horse Teeth, barely able to keep the drool out of her voice.

'Yeah. He usually pops in here about eight,' Horsy had said.

Rachel knew that Michelle had ticked Craig's name as the next one on her list of victims of her fatal charm. Michelle knew that Rachel would scratch her eyes out if she made a move, because she'd had him on her hit list for weeks. But, so what? Rachel was in the Ladies. Michelle was plodding through the cobblestones on Church Walk and wincing, barely two minutes' away from Degsy's.

*

Rachel burst through the door of Degsy's bistro and panted up to the counter.

'Any sign of Craig Eddlestone?' she breathed to Horse Teeth.

'It's only five to. Where's your fat friend to-night?' he asked conversationally.

'At the pictures,' she smirked.

'So, what'll it be?' Horse Teeth asked.

'A small Coke, and a tall hunk, please,' she giggled. 'But I'll just go and check on my looks. Want to be at my best tonight.'

'Actually,' Horse Teeth mused, 'you look like streaky bacon. Is that fake tan?'

'Thanks very much!' Rachel snarled, bristling away to the loo.

Michelle panted into Degsy's with her shoes in her hand, and fell into the nearest seat, behind a pillar so that Horse Teeth couldn't see her. Horse Teeth fancied her something rotten, and tonight she had bigger fish to fry.

'Coke, please,' she panted to a passing waiter.

'D'you want me to fill them both up?' the waiter sniggered, pointing to the pair of collapsing shoes that she'd plonked on the table.

'Excuse me,' Emma stammered, tapping the police-man on his shoulder. 'But a friend of mine went into the Ladies here quarter of an hour ago, and she hasn't come out. And yes, before you ask, I *have* been in to look for her, but the place is empty.'

'She must have left by the Church Street exit,' the policeman suggested.

'That's what I thought,' Emma said, sadly. 'I just hoped I was wrong. We've missed the start of the film now. Why couldn't she've told me if she wanted to opt out of *Little Dorrit*? I'd've gone on my own.'

'Yeah. I wouldn't mind seeing that myself,' the policeman said. He grinned at her. 'Listen, I'm off duty tomorrow, maybe you'd like to . . . er . . .'

Emma blushed.

'Really?' she asked.

She felt so embarrassed, asking him for help, and then him turning round and being that boy who'd left school last summer, the one with the wicked eyes that everyone liked.

'Tell you what,' he said, taking off his helmet. 'I'm officially off duty at eight, and I usually go into this little café for a cold drink. Why don't I buy you one, too? You're Emma Lawrence, aren't you? I remember you from school. One of the quiet ones . . . Oh, I don't mean any offence by that. If you remember, I was one of the quiet ones myself. And you used to go round with that awful Michelle Hawkes and that ferret-faced girl. What's her name?'

'Um . . . Rachel . . .' Emma gulped.

'That's her. Not your type really, were they?' the policeman smiled, his eyes twinkling, steering her up Church Street, along Church Walk to the brightly painted frontage of the café. 'Oh, I'm Craig Eddlestone by the way.'

'Yes, I know,' Emma blushed, letting him open the door for her.

And, together, they stepped into Degsy's, smiling at each other, neither of them noticing the streaky ferret in the short white dress coming out of the loo, or the panting, plump, shoeless girl sobbing behind a pillar.

Another Kind of Pain

The worst holiday in my life was when we went to Majorca.

Whenever I mention that, someone always says, 'But I thought you'd never been to Majorca?' and I say, 'That's right.' Because we never made it to the airport. And that's why it was the worst holiday of my life.

It was an October half-term break, one of those cheap special deals, and I was really looking forward to it because things hadn't been too brilliant at home, and we'd had a really dismal summer at our caravan in Wales because Dad couldn't get away from work to join us, and it had rained non-stop, and Jim, my brother, was waiting for his A level results, so he was irritable and my mother was even more irritable. The inside of the caravan was perpetually steamed up with rows, and Jim kept going on about how he'd be glad to get away from all this, and why did we have to go on holiday with parents anyway? Then I got into trouble for staying out as late as he did.

Anyway, this October break was supposed to put all that behind us. Jim had gone off to college so I was all on my own, and because Mum and Dad were a bit funny with each other they were all over me, and in some ways I was getting a good deal out of it all. In some ways.

I have to admit, I'd heard the rumours. Our town is small enough and gossipy enough for news to spread from one side to the other within a week, and only a deaf man wouldn't have heard that something was going on between my dad and this woman from Willowbank. But I'd thought that nothing would jerk us all out of the rut we were in. I thought that nothing ever really changes. Not dramatically, anyway.

But I was wrong.

On the night before the holiday we'd packed and put the cases all neatly in the hall, then gone out for a meal to McDonald's because Mum likes to leave the house squeaky clean and disinfected when we go away, and she didn't want to mess up the cooker by making a meal.

Dad was really quiet in McDonald's, even quieter than he'd been for the last few months, but I tried to ignore it because I was so excited.

Anyway, we went back home to sleep until five o'clock when the taxi was coming to take us to the airport. I went upstairs and got all settled down, and then I was woken up.

It must have been three or four o'clock in the morning when the row got noisy enough to disturb me. I lay stiffly, breathing shallowly and listening for almost an hour. Then, when I looked at the clock and saw it was almost half-past four I didn't really know what to do. The row was still blazing. Dad kept saying the same thing over and over again, that there was no way he could go on, that he wasn't coming on holiday, and that he was leaving, to move in with Marion Goldshaw. He kept telling Mum that she had to take me to Majorca, and she kept saying that there was no way we were leaving without him, not this time.

By quarter to five I was crying. The tears were huge and silent and were soaked up by the duvet that I held just beneath ear level. I knew Majorca was something that just wasn't going to happen now.

At five o'clock the taxi came and the driver peeped his horn, then came and bashed at the door until my dad finally had to tell him that he wasn't needed. There was another argument until Dad gave him some money, then came back in, and the row with Mum went on. At seven, exhausted and rattled by sobs which no longer produced any tears, I dressed and crept down to sit on the stairs.

I don't know what it was that made me need to listen to the row. The best thing to have done would have been to close my ears to the whole thing. But just as I'd done so many times before, I sat and listened and hated both of them for saying things to each other which I believed I could never forgive, even if they ever kissed and made up.

At eight my dad left, slamming out of the house, and ten minutes later, so did I. I hurled myself down the stairs when I heard the car engine start, and fell over the suitcases which were still parked in the hall with the bright little labels attached.

'Where's my dad gone?' I screamed at my mum.

She just kept on crying, and shrugged.

'Are we going to Majorca or not?' I asked, and she said, 'What do you think?'

She was so pathetic. She'd given way and given in. How could she ever stand up for me if she hadn't been able to stand up for herself? But she didn't stop me running out after Dad, which she probably saw as a pointless gesture. It was, of course. But you make pointless gestures just to show how you feel, knowing all the time that you're not going to be able to influence the outcome by what you do. I ran after the car, ten minutes after the car had left, when it was miles out of sight, and I cried and called his name, and that felt pointless but right.

After a while, the emotional storm died down and thought began to take over, slowing my steps, dictating my direction. I knew this woman lived in Willowbank. I knew her name because I'd heard Mum shouting it at Dad hysterically. I could ask where she lived, if necessary. But I didn't want to do that. I didn't want to talk to anyone and I didn't want to say the name. There were other ways. I walked the length of Willowbank, past the arcade of shops, past the park, the blocks of flats, the rows of neat semis until I saw his car parked.

I'd walked about five miles. It must have been about eleven by this time. It was a Saturday and Willowbank, a main road leading eventually to the town centre, was, by mid-morning, packed with noisy traffic and busy shoppers, kids going to the ice-rink and park, and slowly chugging buses.

My dad's car was in the driveway of a small, bright, terraced house, one of those modern ones with flat little windows, built in blocks of four.

I was exhausted. I hadn't eaten, hadn't slept, hadn't had a single positive happy thought in my head for twelve hours or more. Now that I was confronted with the proof that my dad had chosen someone else to live with, I didn't know what to do. I was empty of everything.

Just opposite the house was one of those flowerbed things with a war memorial and benches all around. I flopped on to a bench and watched my dad's car. I couldn't think what else to do. Eventually I found myself looking up at the windows of the house. One of the front bedrooms had pink frilly blinds – I've always hated those things – but the window next to it, the small one, had red curtains and there were things on the windowsill: stuffed toys, paperback books piled at a drunken angle, a bright yellow radio-cassette player.

Then the front door opened and a girl came out, a girl about my age. She was dressed in a navy sweater and jeans, and she waved at someone who was padlocking a bike to the park railings beside me, then came running across the road.

It's difficult to describe exactly how I felt at that moment, seeing that girl. You see, as far as I'd imagined the picture, my father had run away to be with another woman. Not another family. Not with another girl, like me. My age, my build, my interests. He'd rejected me in favour of another who looked, to my biased eyes, at any rate, not quite as attractive as I was.

The pain was almost unbearable. I watched as this other me, this better-than-me whom my father had selected as his new daughter, raced into the arms of the boy with the bike, and I couldn't say a word. I couldn't react, because this went above and beyond all feeling. All small rejections and refusals in my life had been just little rehearsals for this terrifying loneliness and self-doubt.

'You've been crying,' the boy murmured to her, flinging his arm round her shoulders.

'He's here. He says he's moving in for good,' she sobbed, burying her head in the boy's shoulder as he led her past me towards the park gates. 'I hate him. I hate him! He's not my real dad! I don't think I can stand it, Simon!'

Her muffled voice faded as the two of them, the

boy supporting her and whispering to her, his hand stroking her hair, went by me, leaving me alone with a stone for a heart and nothing in my head.

And then the reaction set in, I suppose. Just as the reaction to hyperactivity is frozen stillness, so my reaction to this feeling of being bludgeoned into emptiness was a kind of propellant fury.

I ran blindly across the road, ignoring the swerving traffic and screaming car horns, and into the driveway where my dad's car sat, innocently, as if it had never been party to his deceptions. I climbed up on to the bonnet and began jumping up and down in my DMs, dementedly. The car was, to my mind, something else my dad cared for, something I could at least attack and perhaps destroy, as he had destroyed me.

A small crowd started to gather. They hung like gnats in the blurred distance, droning and buzzing excitedly. The bedroom window, the one with the blinds, was pushed open, and a woman's voice screamed. 'Derek! Look! It's your daughter!'

I remember my dad coming out, in his shirt sleeves and bare feet, and this woman – a plumper, darker, smaller version of my mum – standing at the front door, holding her dressing gown up tight round her throat and staring with huge scared eyes as he tried to talk me down and reason with me. It wasn't that I wouldn't stop. I couldn't stop. It was as simple and as complicated as that. I kept thinking about how he'd left without even saying goodbye for a life that he thought was mysteriously better than the one Mum and I had given him. He hadn't said goodbye. He'd found another daughter and hadn't told me or explained why.

I fell exhausted finally on the roof of the car, and a policeman pulled me gently down from there.

I wouldn't let my father touch me. They drove me home in their car, with my father following in his dented Escort, and I was asleep before we arrived back and had to be carried back in to where my mother waited nervously to put me to bed, and my dad cried and said sorry.

As I said, it was the worst holiday in my life, the one when we almost went to Majorca. It was an incident which they keep telling me is best forgotten.

'Pretend it never happened,' Mum says.

The next year we went to Florida, all four of us, Mum, Dad, Jim and I, and stayed for a month. We had a really great time, in a way, because Mum and Dad were all sorted out and happy again. But in another way nothing's ever as great as when you're a little kid, before you grow up to discover that choosing to love can mean choosing to hurt, and before someone you love has chosen, accidentally, to hurt you.

THE END

If you would like to receive a Newsletter about our new Children's books, just fill in the coupon below with your name and address (or copy it onto a separate piece of paper if you don't want to spoil your book) and send it to:

The Children's Books Editor
Transworld Publishers Ltd.
61–63 Uxbridge Road
Ealing
London W5 5SA

Please send me a Children's Newsletter:

Name _Leanne Cunniffe_

Address _14 Spernin Close,_

Tamlaght Rd

Omagh

(D) Tyrone

_N. I_

_BT78 5DL_

All Children's Books are available at your bookshop or newsagent, or can be ordered from the following address:

Transworld Publishers Ltd.
Cash Sales Department,
P.O. Box 11, Falmouth, Cornwall TR10 9EN

Please send a cheque or postal order (no currency) and allow 80p for postage and packing for the first book plus 20p for each additional book ordered up to a maximum charge of £2.00 in UK.

B.F.P.O. customers please allow 80p for the first book and 20p for each additional book.

Overseas customers, including Eire, please allow £1.50 for postage and packing for the first book, £1.00 for the second book, and 30p for each subsequent title ordered.